For a minute, Melanie was seventeen again and caught  **the shadows of the high school bleach** **her and turned he**

Even now, almost a de ... on her. She wasn't he... She put her hands between them—damn, when did his chest get so solid and muscular—and pushed hard, stepping back as she did, and colliding with the ladder. Before she caved to more than just a kiss. "What was that?"

He grinned. "A kiss. Unless it's been so long, you've forgotten what it's like to be kissed by me?"

She definitely hadn't forgotten that. "That wasn't part of catching up."

"I'm sorry. I must have misread you."

He hadn't misread her, not one bit. In fact, every single nerve and hormone in her body had been leaning toward Harris, begging for a kiss. The logical side of her brain, however, was the party pooper who'd reminded her that she was here for a job, not a one-night stand with a man she'd never truly forgotten. Yet another reason to keep this light and breezy and focus on the story, not on the man.

* * *

THE STONE GAP INN...
Where Love Comes Home.

Dear Reader,

Thank you for returning to the Stone Gap Inn! This month's read is all about the lies we tell others and the lies we tell ourselves about what our lives are really like.

Melanie Cooper has become a master at pretending everything is fine. But she's really deceiving everyone around her—because she doesn't want her family to worry that her seemingly perfect life isn't so perfect anymore.

We've all done that, I think, at one time or another in our lives. Social media, very often, is a fictitious portrait of our lives, a snippet of time where everything is fabulous, the house is clean and the kids are behaving perfectly. I don't know about you, but I think I've had maybe five seconds total where all those things aligned at the same time!

Life is messy, and these characters in Stone Gap slowly come to realize that being messy is totally okay. That it's perfectly acceptable to not have all your ducks in a row, and to admit that, every now and then, you need a little help. So take a couple hours to put up your feet, let the laundry wait a bit, and have a cup of tea and a fun read. I'll be doing the same at my house, because sometimes there are way more important things in the world than dust bunnies.

Happy reading!

Shirley

Their Last
Second Chance

———

Shirley Jump

HARLEQUIN® SPECIAL EDITION

Recycling programs
for this product may
not exist in your area.

ISBN-13: 978-1-335-57404-6

Their Last Second Chance

Printed in U.S.A.

New York Times and *USA TODAY* bestselling author **Shirley Jump** spends her days writing romance so she can avoid the towering stack of dirty dishes, eat copious amounts of chocolate and reward herself with trips to the mall. Visit her website at shirleyjump.com for author news and a book list, and follow her at Facebook.com/shirleyjump.author for giveaways and deep discussions about important things like chocolate and shoes.

Books by Shirley Jump

Harlequin Special Edition

The Stone Gap Inn

The Family He Didn't Expect

The Barlow Brothers

The Firefighter's Family Secret
The Tycoon's Proposal
The Instant Family Man
The Homecoming Queen Gets Her Man

Harlequin Romance

The Christmas Baby Surprise
The Matchmaker's Happy Ending
Mistletoe Kisses with the Billionaire
Return of the Last McKenna
How the Playboy Got Serious
One Day to Find a Husband
Family Christmas in Riverbend
The Princess Test
How to Lasso a Cowboy

Visit the Author Profile page
at Harlequin.com for more titles.

To my editor, Susan Litman, for loving the Barlows and Stone Gap just as much as I do, and for making every single book the best it can be.

Chapter One

Melanie Cooper told her first lie at the age of five. Or, at least, the first lie she remembered. She'd been playing in the creek a quarter mile away from home—a forbidden destination, but too tempting to avoid. The creek was her favorite place in the entire world, chock-full of crawdads and little minnows that flickered like silver coins.

She'd heard her mother calling her and had run for the hole in the fence, hoping to sneak in as if she'd never left. Her knee connected with the fence, and by the time she'd scrambled into the yard, the gash had become a geyser. When her mother asked her why she had taken so long to come in, Melanie had made up an elaborate story about a lost puppy and tripping over the curb trying to bring him back to his owner. Her mother had ignored the leaving-the-yard violation and made a big deal about Melanie's big heart, delivering a rare dose of praise. In that moment, Melanie had learned that lying was the best way to get out of trouble—and win her hypercritical mother's approval.

So it stood to reason that she would end up working at *City Girl* magazine, where lying was part of the job description. She spent her days writing articles about how to lose twenty pounds in ten days, filling them with tips like *drink green tea, grab an extra workout, take the stairs at work*, and the editor would plop a miracle-promising title on the cover and sell twenty percent more copies to all those people wanting instant weight-loss results.

As she pulled into Stone Gap, North Carolina, heading down Main Street and across town to her sister Abby's house, Melanie knew she was going to have to be extra convincing when she lied to Abby. Her older sister wasn't some gullible reader in the grocery store looking for the untold secret to erasing cellulite. She was smart, and she knew Melanie well. Too well. If Melanie's story faltered one bit, Abby would see the truth.

And the last thing she wanted Abby to know was that Melanie's hard-won perfect life had fallen apart.

Her throat closed, and she forced herself to take in a deep breath. Another. It would be okay. She'd turn this around, somehow. Plus, she had a job offer waiting for her at a prestigious online news magazine, if she could prove that she had the chops to write about more than just diets and mascara. That's why she didn't need to tell Abby—all would be set to rights again soon. Besides, Abby was getting married next weekend, and she had Ma staying with her, which was a herculean task unto itself. The last thing Abby needed to worry about was her little sister's latest crisis.

Or cris*es*, plural, considering she'd lost her marriage, her home and her job in relatively quick succession. Melanie's entire life had become a string of empty promises and false leads, as if working in a fiction-creating world had colored her own reality.

Melanie took a right, then swung down the tree-lined cul-de-sac and into the driveway of Abby's bungalow. It was the perfect little house, ringed by red geraniums and decorated with a porch swing that made a lazy arc in the breeze. A blue bicycle leaned in the shade of an oak tree, and a football waited in the sun for a game of catch. The fall air carried a sense of home as foreign to Melanie as a nor'easter to a Floridian. Years ago, she'd thought—

Well, it didn't matter. Years ago was done and over.

Melanie tipped down the mirror, checked her makeup, then straightened her T-shirt and brushed invisible lint off her jeans before she got out of the car and strode up the stairs.

Jacob came running out of the house first, wearing a Transformers T-shirt in bright yellow that made him look like a minibus. "Aunt Melanie!" He barreled into her legs.

Melanie let out an oomph, then bent down and swung her five-year-old nephew up and into her arms. "How's the best Jacob in the world?"

"I'm playing soccer! Mommy says I'm really good. And Dylan is my coach and we have lots of fun and we won our first game!"

Melanie laughed. "That's awesome, buddy. Goodness, you're getting big." She lowered him to the ground—her nephew seemed to have grown six inches and added twenty pounds since the last time she saw him two Christmases ago. He slid his little hand into hers and pulled her up the stairs and into the house, talking nonstop the whole time about school, soccer and his new puppy. The simple affection of Jake's tiny fingers in hers tugged at Melanie's heartstrings. Emotion choked her throat, but she pushed it away just as she entered the kitchen.

Abby was pulling something out of the oven. She set the casserole pan on the stove top, then turned, a ready smile on her face. "Melanie! You're here. How was the drive? I can't believe you drove all the way from New York."

A yellow lab puppy scrambled to his feet and bounded across the kitchen, all feet and tail, before skidding to a stop in front of Melanie. "That's Dudley," Jake said. "He's got a dinosaur name."

"A dinosaur name?" The puppy nudged Melanie's hand, his tail thwapping on the floor.

"Yup. My dentist, Dr. Corbett, gave me a book 'cause I was so good when I got my teeths cleaned. And the book had Dudley the Dinosaur in it. But he wasn't a scary dinosaur. He's not the kind that can bite you. He's the kind that eats his vegetables. And brushes his teeth."

Melanie laughed. "Sounds like a very smart dinosaur and a very good name for a dog."

"Dylan got him for us." Jake hugged the dog's neck and kissed his forehead.

"Well, he's adorable." Melanie set her purse in an empty chair, then set her phone on the table. No calls, no texts, no miracles on the notification screen. That was okay. Just walking into Abby's house eased some of the tension in Melanie's shoulders.

"He's trouble is what he is," Abby said with a laugh. Undoubtedly, she was taking the puppy in stride, as she did everything else. Abby had always had this easy casualness about her, in the way she looked, the way she parented, the way she got through life. Today, her brown hair was back in a loose ponytail, and she was wearing a pale lime V-neck T-shirt with dark blue skinny jeans. A small round diamond sparkled on her left hand. Abby smiled, a genuine glad-to-see-you smile, but Melanie could see the strain in Abby's eyes, the stress of the last few days since their mother had arrived. "You got the entire fur-and-little-person welcoming committee."

"And got to hear all about soccer, the puppy and how much he likes his teacher, just in the walk down the hall." Melanie ruffled Jacob's hair. "Sounds like he's been a busy boy."

"*Busy* should have been his middle name." Abby opened her arms and drew Melanie into a tight hug. "I've missed you."

"I've missed you, too." Melanie held on a little longer to Abby than Abby held on to her. A part of Melanie wanted to open up, to let the tears fall, to tell Abby the truth. Maybe she should. Maybe Abby would have just the right words of wisdom. "Oh, and congratulations again. I'm so happy for you."

"Thank you. Dylan really is an amazing man. I'm incredibly happy to be marrying him."

When Melanie drew back, she caught the joy in Abby's eyes, matching the sparkle of the ring on her finger, and Melanie couldn't do it. All her life, Abby had been the one to protect Melanie, to bandage her wounds when she fell down, to comfort her when a date stood her up, to bail her out when she got in trouble. How could she dim the look in Abby's eyes? Tell her that her finally well-adjusted, settled little sister had completely upended everything?

Again.

Melanie couldn't bear to see the look of disappointment that would follow. Those eyes that would say *here we go again* and be followed by constant fretting and advice. She'd thought—they'd *both* thought—that those times were behind them. The days when Melanie was brought home by the cops for underage drinking or caught skipping school or sneaking home at three in the morning were in the past.

Back then, Abby had been the one to cover for her sister, to sit Melanie down, time after time, and stress the importance of graduating high school, going to college, getting a job, being responsible. It had taken a couple years for the message to sink in, and even then Melanie had slipped off the path more than once, coming close to ending up in jail and nearly making a decision that would have ruined her life. *Slow to grow up* was what her mother had called her, and maybe Ma was right. But she really thought she'd done it—that she'd figured out the rule book and been rewarded with success. It had all been perfect…until it wasn't. Because here Melanie was at twenty-nine, alone, jobless and adrift.

Not exactly a shoo-in for the Most Successful award at the next high school reunion.

"So…how's Ma?" Melanie asked, then lowered her voice. "Driving you nuts?"

Abby sighed. "She's retired now and bored, and telling the whole world about how terrible her life is. I love her, Mel, but…"

"She sucks all the fun out of the room like a social vampire?"

"Exactly." Abby laughed. "Anyway, Ma is taking a nap right now. She should be down for dinner."

Just as well. That gave Melanie a little more time to avoid the double sister-mother inquisition. Together, they might be able to ferret out the truth. "How's the wedding planning going? And please don't tell me you're one of those brides who is filling tiny Mason jars with homemade jam and sending a dressed-up baby goat down the aisle? Because I wrote a story about that, and I'm just saying, goat wrangler is not part of my maid of honor duties."

Abby laughed, slid a cookie sheet filled with biscuits into the oven and then stirred a pan of vegetables, while Jake peeled off and headed for the living room and a mountain of Legos on the carpet. "Not quite. But I do hope stress reduction is something you do, because the caterer got the flu, so I had to find someone else, and the band has dropped off the face of the earth. Thank God Meri Barlow is helping me. She's photographing the wedding and has been a great resource for finding replacement people, like her sister-in-law Rachel, who is a part-time wedding planner. I swear, planning a wedding is more stressful than being a mom."

"Well, you don't have to add worrying about me to that list. I'm great. Couldn't be better." Yep, lying in person was almost as easy as lying in print. Maybe she could write an article about that. Except she no longer had a job at a magazine and nowhere to publish something like "Ten Tips for Hiding Failure from Your Family."

"And Adam? How's he?"

"He's…good. Busy with work. Said he'd try to visit next time." She hadn't seen her ex-husband in over a year, when she'd sat across from him in the judge's chambers and signed her name on the final divorce decree. He and his pretty face and magazine-ready smile had walked away without a backward glance. Last she knew, he was living in a condo in the Bronx with Cheri, the twenty-one-year-old receptionist at his agent's office. One of those girls who put a smiley face over the *i* in her name was prone to giggling fits.

Melanie had been intending to tell her sister and mother about her divorce. But she hadn't been able to find the words, especially when Ma went on and on about how proud she was of her married writer daughter. It had been easier to continue pretending everything was fine than to admit her life had been crumbling for a long time. That she'd gone back to being the family failure.

"You know, you don't have to stay at the inn," Abby said. "I can put Jake into Cody's room and Cody can take the couch if you want to take his bed. It'll be a little cramped, but they're boys. They'll be fine. Besides, between school and work, Cody is hardly ever here."

Staying here and disrupting Abby's teenage son, as well as little Jake, would mean seeing her mother at all hours, not to mention talking to Abby on a daily basis. Melanie could only keep up the *everything's fine* charade so long. Doing it from breakfast to bedtime would be impossible. And though she could ill afford the room fee for the inn, she knew staying there would make it possible to keep the truth from becoming obvious. "Aw, thanks, sis, but I'll be fine. I've got some work to do, anyways, so even if I stayed here, I'd be holed up in my room most of the time. I'm sure you have a zillion things to do for the wedding, and this way, you won't have to worry about me, too."

Abby cocked her head and studied her little sister. Melanie held her ground and put a bright smile on her face. *Everything's fine, everything's fine.*

"Okay, if that's what you want. But if you change your mind, you always have a place here," Abby said.

"Thanks." Melanie gave Abby a quick hug. "You're the best."

They got busy setting the table, with Jake buzzing around the oval shape like an airplane and Dudley nipping at his heels. Cody ambled in a few minutes later, followed by Dylan, Abby's fiancé. The last time Melanie had seen Cody, he'd been a sullen, withdrawn teenager, angry at the world. Today, the seventeen-year-old walked in with a smile on his face, ready with a hug for his mom and then one for his aunt. "Hey, Aunt Melanie. How was your trip?"

She blinked back her surprise. Cody was engaging with adults? To her shock, there was no trace of the teenage angst she'd seen when Abby and the boys had visited New York a couple years ago. Clearly, settling down in Stone Gap and adding Dylan to their family had been a good influence on the boys. "Great. Thanks. I hear you're working at the community center now."

"Yup. Dylan's got me doing some maintenance," Cody said, his face filled with pride and excitement, a mirror to Jake's earlier, "and helping out with the basketball program. We're planning a job fair kind of thing for next month, too."

"He's practically running the place now." Dylan grinned and clapped a hand on Cody's shoulder. Dylan was a tall, lanky man with brown hair and a ready smile. He clearly loved Abby and the boys, and Abby loved him, given the joy that lit her face as soon as Dylan walked into the room. Any man who made her older sister that happy got Melanie's immediate stamp of approval.

Cody blushed and ducked his head. "I'm just helping."

"Well, you're doing a great job."

While Melanie exchanged small talk with her nephews and Dylan, Abby excused herself, went upstairs, then came back a few minutes later. "Ma isn't feeling well, Mel. She asked if you'd bring her a plate and then you two can visit. I think she got too much sun today, walking downtown with me. We got lunch and planned on some window shopping, but…" Abby shrugged.

"Ma complained about the noise and the heat and you gave up?" Melanie said. "I get it, sis. I'll take her some dinner."

"Thanks. It's been a stressful few days, and right now…well, I appreciate it. We'll wait until you come back down so we can eat with you." Abby filled a plate with chicken and potatoes, then gave Melanie a set of silverware and a napkin. "First room on the right."

"Thanks." Melanie swallowed her nerves, then climbed the stairs to face her harshest critic.

Cynthia Cooper was a strong woman—anyone who met her would walk away saying exactly that. She'd raised two girls alone, after their father had died in a car accident when Melanie was a baby, and for years she'd worked two jobs to support her family. She'd weathered widowhood, financial crises, a cancer scare and a dozen other issues with a stiff upper lip. To the outside world, she was the epitome of strength. To Melanie, strong was just a euphemism for high expectations with no warm fuzzies.

Melanie knocked on the open door, then stepped into the room. "Hi, Ma. I brought you some dinner."

"It's about time you came and said hello." Her mother sat up in bed, and had arranged the pillows to keep her back straight. For being in her late fifties, Cynthia had aged well, thanks to regular yoga sessions, fastidious application of night creams and unrelenting attention to every aspect of her appearance at all times. She kept her hair dyed blond, wore minimal makeup and even in bed had her hair curled and wore recently pressed pajamas.

Melanie put the plate on a floral bed tray sitting on the ottoman, then set the tray over her mother's lap. "Abby made chicken and potatoes. It smells amazing."

"Hopefully your sister didn't burn this dinner. Last night's was atrocious." Cynthia shook her head. "I swear, it's like you girls haven't retained a single thing I taught you when you were young."

Melanie bit back her first reply, about how hard it was to pay attention to a parent who criticized more than she taught. "Not all of us are good at cooking, Ma."

"Clearly not. I suppose you'd say that you are good at ordering takeout." Another head shake. "Such a waste, especially in today's world, when you can easily eat at home."

Melanie put a smile on her face, because she'd never win the battle over ordering Chinese food versus making her own pot roast. "So, how have you been?"

"Terrible. This heat is killing me. I can't wait to go back to Connecticut, where the weather is reasonable." Ma waved a hand at the air in the room. "It's positively stifling. I can hardly breathe."

North Carolina could get hot, but today had been in the mid-seventies, with low humidity and partial cloud cover. In Ma's room, a ceiling fan spun a lazy circle, and the breeze danced with the edges of the open curtains. "Well, I'll let you eat your dinner," Melanie said.

"Stay." Ma patted the side of the bed. "Visit with your mother for once. You live one state away and I have to go all the way to North Carolina to see you for five minutes."

Melanie perched on the edge of the bed. Her mother speared a piece of chicken and ate it. She tried to think of something she could say that her mother wouldn't turn into a criticism. "Abby's pretty excited about the wedding. And Dylan seems like a really great guy." Maybe if Melanie focused enough attention on her sister, Ma wouldn't think to ask about Melanie's life.

"Yes, far better than that loser she married the first time." Ma made a face. "Anyway, enough about Abby. What have you been up to? Have you been promoted to editor yet? You really should be, you know. You've put in enough time at that magazine."

"Uh, no promotion yet. And I'm doing fine."

"And Adam? How is he? When are you two going to give me a grandchild? Your sister has already had two children."

"I'm aware of how many children Abby has, Ma." How long had she been in the room? Five minutes? Already, her patience had worn thinner than a piece of paper. "I'm not ready to have kids."

"Well, you need to start thinking about these things. You aren't getting any younger. And once you lose your figure, men won't be so interested in making babies with you."

Melanie got to her feet and worked another smile to her face. "Your dinner is going to get cold if we keep talking. We'll visit later."

Like ten years from now, she thought as she headed out of the room and back downstairs. Maybe by then she'd have done all the things that checked off approval on her mother's list.

Somehow, Melanie doubted that. From the minute she'd been born, Melanie had been a runner-up to Abby, and if her mother knew the truth, Melanie wouldn't even be running a close second to her sister, who clearly had it all.

Melanie returned to the sound of happy chatter in the dining room. Jake was telling everyone about his day at school with Cody interjecting with comments about work and Abby and Dylan filling in the blanks. The puppy sat to the side, tail swishing against the floor. The room was filled with the merry sounds of a family.

As happy as Melanie was for her sister, who deserved a good man after divorcing the ex from hell—about that, her mother was right—a part of Melanie was jealous. Maybe things might have worked themselves out if Adam and she had tried for kids...

Wishful thinking. Actually, it was more like unproductive, *stupid* wishful thinking. Adam had turned out to be a self-involved, cheating jerk—the fact that he was a model should have been her first clue that he might be more narcissistic than considerate—and if they'd had kids, she would have wound up tied to him for the rest of her life, in one way or another.

Either way, Adam was out of her life, and if he stayed with Cheri or Shari or whoever she was, he was probably going to make babies who'd have names that would be dotted with little hearts.

Except there'd been a moment when she was eighteen when she had imagined a future with a baby, a husband. A totally different man than the one she married, a man who had made her feel like the most special person on earth—until he'd shattered her heart and the future she'd pictured fell apart.

"Melanie, what do you think?"

She drew herself back to Abby's question. "Uh, sorry. I was daydreaming."

Abby laughed. "Probably thinking about work. How's that going, anyway? I saw the latest issue of *City Girl* when I was at the market. I looked for an article by you, but didn't see one." Abby turned to Dylan. "Melanie writes for a women's magazine. I'm so proud of her, because she grew up to be exactly what she wanted to be."

"Yep, exactly." Unemployed and with a résumé filled with frivolous articles—that was every girl's dream, right? Melanie had been writing ever since she learned how to hold a pencil. She'd once thought she would grow up to be someone writing important things that people would read and remember. She wouldn't call 750 words on mastering under-eye concealer an important thing. She'd taken the first job out of college that offered a steady paycheck and had told herself that it made her happy. At least, it had until last year.

"I didn't have anything in the last issue because I've been, uh, busy researching a big piece." Yeah, researching a job that would pay enough for an unemployed writer to afford New York City rent. Even in a sublet with rent control, Melanie had blown through almost all of her savings. She needed to secure that job at the hard-news online magazine by the end of the month or she'd be eating ramen noodles for every meal for the foreseeable future. The editor at the online magazine had said *bring me something worth publishing and I'll hire you*, but thus far, Melanie hadn't found anything that fit what he was looking for.

"Too bad you don't live here." Dylan took a second helping of chicken, then added a buttered roll. "Saul Richardson, who puts out the *Stone Gap Gazette*, just lost his only writer. He's getting up there in age, and he's totally overwhelmed with writing all the articles himself, along with doing the layout and the printing and distribution. He's been looking for a new journalist but hasn't found one yet."

Melanie's interest perked. Given the size of the town, the *Stone Gap Gazette* likely had a budget far lower than the multimillion-dollar one at *City Girl*. But then again, the cost of living in this North Carolina town was also far lower. She had no interest in taking on a permanent job here, but maybe she could get some work for the next couple weeks, at least until the wedding was over and Abby was off on her honeymoon. That way, Melanie could start adding more than she was subtracting from her checking account. And buy herself some time to come up with that great idea the other editor wanted. "Maybe he would let me write an article or two. Might be fun to do a piece while I'm here."

Abby leaned over and cut a big piece of chicken into smaller bites for Jacob. "It'd be pretty cool to see an article written by my sister in the local paper. I can buy a hundred copies and run around town bragging about you."

Melanie's cheeks heated. She'd known her sister bought the magazine, and she would often text or email about Melanie's latest article. But she'd never imagined her older, accomplished, never-got-in-trouble sister would be that proud. "Thanks, Abs."

"I'm just glad you're here," Abby said. "I didn't think you could get that much time off. Adam must be missing you like crazy. Adam is Mel's husband," she explained to Dylan.

"I couldn't stand to be away from Abby for eight hours, never mind eight days." Dylan met his fiancée's gaze with a tender, quiet connection. "But then again, I'm still in head-over-heels-for-her mode."

Abby laughed. "You've been in that mode since the day you met me."

He gave her a soft, special smile. "That's because you're amazing."

"Ugh. You guys, there are children at the table," Cody said, but a hint of a smile played on his lips.

Melanie had never looked at Adam that way, and he'd

never looked at her like that, either. She'd married him because she'd thought she should, because they'd been dating for two years and it seemed to be the expected thing, the next rung up the respectable-life ladder.

Dylan passed the rolls to Cody and snagged another one for himself. "One of these days, Code, you'll be just as crazy over a girl."

Cody glanced at his mother and then his soon-to-be stepfather. "Yeah, maybe."

There was such happiness here, such a beautiful sense of family, and it seemed sacrilegious to bring falseness into that. But Melanie didn't know any other way to operate, any means of untangling the web she had woven over the past couple of years. The continual stories about her fake happiness with a husband who was gone, about her successes at a job she had already lost, had become so big, all Melanie could do was hope she left town before the edges frayed.

"I should get back to the inn and get checked in," Melanie said. She got to her feet and picked up her half-empty plate. "Sorry to eat and run, Abs, but I have an article to work on tonight."

"Oh, I hate to see you go, too." Abby took the plate from Melanie, then drew her into a hug. "But we have all week to get caught up, and it'll be such a welcome break from the stress of Ma being here and trying to get the wedding details sorted. I plan on spending lots of time with you, little sister. I want to hear all about your adventures in New York, the crazy people you've been interviewing and how that hot husband of yours is sweeping you off your feet."

Melanie's smile wavered. "Sounds great," she said. If nothing else, it would be interesting. It was going to be like reading a novel without scanning the back cover first—she had no idea how the story was going to turn out.

Chapter Two

The Comeback Bar was tucked on a little side street in downtown Stone Gap. Country music poured from the open front door, currently blasting a well-done cover of a Blake Shelton hit. The place sounded inviting, even though from the outside the Comeback looked like it needed a comeback of its own. The gray siding was cracked and faded, the sign above the door was missing a few letters, and a poster tacked to the outside advertising a New Year's Eve party was more than two years out of date.

So maybe this idea didn't bode as well as Melanie had thought. But given the size of Stone Gap, there was only a handful of choices for nightlife. There was the Sea Shanty near the beach, a downtown diner that only stayed open late on Friday nights and the Comeback Bar. Either way, having a drink here was better than sitting in her room at the Stone Gap Inn, alone with her regrets. She'd done that after she checked in and lasted maybe an hour before the urge to leave overwhelmed her.

Melanie ducked inside the bar. It was still in the seventies, a warm night for late September, but Melanie had brought a lightweight sweater anyway, more conditioned to the cooler New York weather than the warmer southern temperatures. She draped her cardigan over the stool next to her, then sat down at the varnished oak bar.

"What can I get you?" A portly guy in a white T-shirt embroidered with the name Al slid a paper coaster her way.

Despite the rundown decor of splintery wood paneling and cracked red vinyl seats, the Comeback Bar had a nice selection of craft beers chalked on a slate board above the bar. Melanie chose an orange wheat one.

"You from out of town?" Al asked as he angled a glass under the tap and pulled the handle.

"Visiting my sister. How'd you know?"

Al set the beer in front of her. He had a wide, friendly face, with a full beard and bushy eyebrows. "This town is smaller than the tip of a pin, so when someone I don't recognize comes in my bar, ninety-nine percent of the time, they're not from here. You staying at the inn?"

"Yes. I just checked in a little while ago." Given that the Stone Gap Inn was literally the only choice within twenty miles of town, Melanie hadn't had a choice, other than staying with perceptive Abby, who would have figured out the truth about Melanie's situation the first night. Besides, Melanie liked the inn, with its Southern charm and view of lush green rolling hills, and most of all she liked Della Barlow and Mavis Beacham, the owners, who were as warm and welcoming as the inn itself. From what she'd been told, Della and Mavis had bought the building a little over a year ago and done a top-to-bottom renovation, adding modern conveniences but keeping the character of the antebellum home, and the historical elements of the 120-year-old two-story house.

Abby had mentioned that when the original Stone Gap Inn, a rather rundown excuse for a hotel, had closed down almost two years ago, Della and Mavis had renovated this antebellum house. They'd been friends with the owner of the first inn, which had been located on the other side of town and kept not only the name, but also the customer list. That was smart business, in Melanie's mind, because it gave the new B&B a built-in clientele from day one. Given how beautifully the restoration had turned out, she was sure the new Stone Gap Inn would be a huge success. The whole place looked like it was out of a movie. Such a change from the concrete world Melanie had left this morning.

"You'll like it at the inn. Della and Mavis run a great place. Since they opened that little place, they've attracted all kinds of folks to our town. Good for them, good for Stone Gap and good for me." Al grinned. "Why, there's one of our newest temporary residents right now. Only been here a few days and already a bona-fide hero."

Melanie turned on the stool. And froze.

Harris McCarthy stood five feet away, all grown-up and handsome as hell. She hadn't seen him in at least eleven years, not since he put her heart through a shredder. They'd grown up in Connecticut and gone to high school together, dated for two years, and as senior year came to a close, they'd talked about forever. Then without warning, he'd broken up with her. On the exact day when she'd needed him most. He hadn't wanted to listen to her, or believe the truth; he'd just ended it and walked away. She'd vowed then and there to never forgive him, to seal her heart against his smile—not that she'd had any expectation of him ever turning that smile her way again. She put a hand over her stomach and reminded herself all over again of that awful, ter-rible summer. What was he doing here, of all places?

Then she remembered what Abby had said when they'd talked a few months ago. That Harris was now a custom builder and he'd been hired to build a house for a baseball player or something in North Carolina. But that had been last year, right?

"Holy hell. Melanie Cooper?" Harris grinned. "Damn. How long has it been?"

"A while." Eleven years, three months and two days. But who counted that kind of thing? Certainly not her, even though the day he'd broken her heart had left her thinking she'd never recover, never move on. "My sister said you were in town building a house or something."

"I was, last year. That project went so well, I've…

uh, had some people asking me to give them quotes, too. So I'm back and making a pit stop for beer." He grinned again, and the part of Melanie that wanted to ignore the past melted a little.

He had a nice smile—always had. The kind that slid across his face as easy as drizzling chocolate on ice cream. He'd been a charmer, class president and captain of the football team and all that, but underneath it all, the Harris she knew was a little shy, introverted. Much happier with a pencil and sketch pad in his hands than a football.

"I'm surprised you became a builder. I thought you were going to be a CPA."

"That was my father's dream, not mine." Harris paused a second. His gaze cut to the beer in his hand. "Turns out I'm happier when I'm working for myself."

Why was she even still talking to him? And what did she care about his career choices? Though she had to admit, builder made better sense than CPA for Harris, who looked nothing like what she pictured when someone said *accountant*. Harris stood just a couple inches over six feet, with straight dark brown hair that had a tendency to sweep against his brow. He'd maintained that quarterback body, all lean and defined and tempting in a dark green V-neck sweater and a pair of worn jeans that whispered comfort and familiarity.

"You down here for Abby's wedding?" Harris asked.

She cocked her head and studied his face. Not the way his chest filled out the sweater and the jeans hugged his legs. "How'd you know my sister's getting married?"

"Harris here knows 'bout everyone in Stone Gap." Al plopped a second paper coaster in front of Harris. "And after Tuesday night, 'bout everyone knows his name, too."

Harris's features shifted from friendly and open to distant and closed. "Al, can I get one of the lagers?"

"Sure." Al turned, filled another glass and handed it to Harris. "Here you go. On the house, considering. You should tell her your story, Harris. What you did—"

"—is over and done, and not up for discussion." Harris raised the beer in Al's direction. "Thanks for the beer, and I *am* paying for it."

Whatever Harris had done that had turned him into a hero in Al's mind was clearly something he didn't want to talk about. That intrigued the reporter in Melanie. She sensed a story underneath the surface, the kind that editors would rush to have.

The kind that could maybe, just maybe, get an unemployed magazine writer a fresh new start.

"I'd love to hear the story," Melanie said, gesturing toward the stool beside her. "If you want to talk about it."

"No, I really don't. But I'll talk about anything else." He nodded at her sweater. "Aren't you expecting someone?"

A part of her had sort of hoped to see a flicker of jealousy on Harris's face, but all she saw was a plain old question. Why did she care what he thought about whether she was alone or waiting for her now-pretend husband? She was over him. *So* over him.

"There's no one sitting there now," she said, pitching her answer into a vague left field. Let him make of that what he wanted. She picked up her sweater and draped it over her lap.

He sat down and spun the stool a little toward her. "It's sure nice to see you here. So, where have you been for the last decade, Mellie?"

Harris was the only human being on the planet who could call her Mellie. He'd done it almost from their first date, and the nickname had stuck. He'd whispered it in her ear when they'd made love for the first time, and she'd heard him say it for the last time, with a hitch in his throat, when he'd told her it was over. *Mellie* rocketed her mind and heart back to stolen kisses in the science hallway, skipping school together once on a lazy spring afternoon and late nights on a blanket under the stars.

She took a sip of her beer, delaying her answer until the memories flitted away and she could draw herself back to the present. To a band singing about a lost love and a man who was no longer part of her world. "I've been working at a magazine in New York."

"A writer? That's great." He gave her a satisfied nod. "And a perfect career for you. You always blew me away with your essays in English. And remember that paper you wrote on the Civil War? The one that told the story of the war from the perspective of a divided family? That was amazing."

"You remember that?"

"I remember a lot of things from those years, Mellie."

She retreated to the beer again, but this time the sip

didn't have the same magic. Her heart fluttered a bit, her pulse raced and she wondered vaguely if Harris kissed the same as he had in high school, or if the years between had made his kisses hotter, deeper, sweeter. What was wrong with her? The man had destroyed her heart that summer. *Stop talking to him.* "And you? What have you been up to?"

"Did the college thing, got that degree in accounting my dad wanted me to get and went to work at the headquarters for PMA in Greenwich."

Melanie nodded her understanding. It was the life she'd expected him to have—chugging away at the massively successful firm his father had grown from a one-man CPA office to a nationwide enterprise. "Did you do taxes or something else?"

"I worked in business consulting," Harris continued. "Really code for helping big companies devour little companies, eliminating competition and driving profits higher. I hated every single second I worked there." He chuckled, but there was a hint of bitterness in his tone. "I started working part-time after hours for a builder, doing manual labor, and found I loved working with my hands. The guy I worked for encouraged me to get my contractor's license, and the day I did, I went into my father's office, quit my job and leaped into the unknown."

"Wow. That's a pretty gutsy move." Though not a big surprise from the football player who had carried the team through two winning years. The same boy who had had a contentious relationship with his father.

"I figured I didn't want to live a life of regrets," Harris said. "After I started working for my father, I became even more certain that I didn't want to end up like him, bitter and angry at the world. He's still so pissed I did it, I think he took me off his Christmas card list." He shook his head, as if that was no big deal, but Melanie remembered Harris's father and knew that when Phillip McCarthy held a grudge, he held it forever. She also detected a note of sadness in Harris's voice. "Anyway, that's pretty much me in a nutshell. These days, I figure I'm blessed to be making decent money at something I love."

"That's great. Really. I'm happy for you." *Walk away from him. Stop asking questions. And don't look at his left hand.*

"Thanks." He set his glass on the polished surface. "Did you get married? Have kids?"

"No kids. And yes, I got married."

Harris's gaze flicked to her empty left hand. "And got unmarried, I presume?"

She could lie. Make up some big story about Adam getting her a new band or something that would explain the lack of a ring on her finger. But Melanie was tired of lying. It had been hard enough to do with her sister, and now, with Harris, whom she probably wouldn't see again anyway and who had no reason to talk to her sister, lying seemed pointless. "Yeah, a year ago, but I haven't really uh…talked about it with my family. You know, not wanting to distract from Abby's happiness and all." Yep, that was her reason for lying to her sister's face. "What about you?"

His left hand was also empty. So, no woman living in some palatial estate with Harris?

"Came close once," he said. "But no wife, no kids."

Came close once. What woman had nearly captured his heart forever? And why did Melanie care? "How long are you in Stone Gap?"

"Until my latest…project is done, which should be…a few weeks or so. That's the great part about my job. Flexibility in hours and location." He took a sip of beer, then put the glass down again and leaned an elbow on the bar. "You know, I'd love to show you the town. It's a great little place. I loved it here the first time and love it just as much now."

"Oh, I'm fine, thanks." She turned back to her beer and took a big gulp. The sooner she finished it, the sooner she could leave. "I'm pretty busy the next week or so anyway. Helping Abby finish up the wedding details and working. You know how it is with deadlines. Always under the gun."

Okay, so she wasn't exactly done lying.

Harris slid a card across the bar to her. "Here's my cell. Call me or text me if you have a little time between cake tastings and headband weaving or whatever bridesmaids do. I really would love to see you again, Mellie."

She pocketed the card, then got to her feet. If she stayed here any longer, the alcohol that was already buzzing her head a bit would lead her to a bad decision. She'd made plenty of those with Harris. "Enjoy your beer. Maybe I'll see you around town."

He grinned. "I'm sure we will see each other again, really soon."

Melanie shook her head. "I'm pretty busy, Harris, I don't think so."

"Like Al said, there's only one place to stay in Stone Gap." He paused, waited for that sentence to sink in, then finished, "Which means you and I are both at the inn."

Damn this small town. Why couldn't it have a seedy motel or a second B&B? What kind of bad luck did a girl have to have to lose her marriage and her job, and then end up stuck in the same cozy inn as her ex-boyfriend?

With Harris at the Stone Gap Inn, they'd undoubtedly run into each other in the halls or at breakfast. Well, she could handle that. This was the man who had broken her heart, after all. She wasn't going to get wrapped up in his *Mellie* spell, not again. "Maybe we'll see each other in passing. Have a good night, Harris."

She turned to go, but then he reached out and touched her. In an instant, all those pretty little resolutions she'd just made disappeared. Her pulse tripped, and her mind rocketed back to the science hall and the moonlight.

"Don't leave, not yet, Mellie." Her name slid through his voice on a soft note. "Have another beer. We can talk, like old times."

She hesitated, then came back to real life and the present day. "I'm not here to reminisce, Harris. And the old times weren't always as good as you think they were."

She shrugged into her coat, which forced his hand to drop away, then she turned on her heel and headed out into a warm night that seemed ten degrees colder and darker.

The clock on Harris's bedside table ticked past midnight. The numbers on the screen before him blurred. He rubbed his temples. Too many hours sitting at this desk on his laptop, trying to work out some estimates for an upcoming project, when his mind was anywhere but on the palatial house he'd been hired to build back in Connecticut. He kept thinking of Mellie, of how amazing she looked, of how much he'd wanted to kiss her.

And of how uninterested she'd seemed in being with him, talking to him, being near him. Of course, they had broken up a long time ago and in a terrible way, but still, for a moment he'd thought he'd seen a flicker of something in her eyes. The same something that had run through him when he recognized her. The same something that had never really died.

It might have been almost a decade since they'd dated, but the second he saw Mellie, it was as if no time at all had passed. Back in high school in Connecticut, where they'd both grown up, they'd been inseparable. Two peas, one pod, her grandmother had called them. He'd started his days back then walking her to school and ended them with long phone calls that would last until one of their parents yelled at them to get to bed.

Now, knowing she was sleeping just down the hall, his concentration had fled. He'd hoped that he'd see her at the inn when he got in from the Comeback, but she had already gone to bed, her door shut, no light shining beneath it. Mavis, the gregarious African American woman who covered the night shift at the inn, had told Harris that Melanie's room was two doors away from his. She was staying in Charleston, and he was in Asheville, as the rooms were named. Close geographically, but given the way she'd walked away from him without a backward glance a couple hours ago, miles apart in every other respect.

He got up, stretched his back, gave the computer one last glance, then shut the lid. Trying to work was a waste of time—and seeing Mellie again was only part of the reason why. He had more on his mind than a woman he'd once loved. And more wrongs to right than the ones from his teenage years. In the morning he'd try again. Maybe by then he'd have chased Mellie from his mind.

He headed downstairs for a snack, something to fill the hours until he got sleepy. And until he could usher that crowd of regrets out of his thoughts.

A single light burned over the kitchen sink, casting the space in a soft golden glow. The rest of the world seemed still and dark, quiet, magical. Harris loved this time of night, with its promise of something new in a few hours. Fresh beginnings and clean slates and all that. Harris believed in those kinds of things—because someone in his family had to.

He grabbed a beer out of the fridge, then headed out to the back deck. Two Adirondack chairs faced the lush landscaping, the deep green hills that rolled down the back and opened to a partial view of Stone Gap Lake. The dark turned the land into a set of unrecognizable shapes, except for the moon winking at the wide oval of the lake.

In the air, he could still catch the scent of smoke, of charred wood, of lives destroyed from just a few days earlier—the so-called heroic event Al had wanted to praise him for. If he closed his eyes, he was back there, in that two-story house, blinded by smoke, deafened by the roar of the flames and the splintering of the beams above his head. He could hear the screams that ebbed by the second, caught in coughs and despair as the house began to crumble around them all. If he'd been two minutes later—

He hadn't been, and for that he was grateful. The Kingston family was grateful, too. Colton Barlow, one of the first on the scene with the Stone Gap Fire Department, had told Harris the entire family—and the nearby homes—were damned lucky that Harris had gotten there so quickly. Harris didn't mention the slurred phone call from John that had set off alarm bells in Harris's head and had him flying across town in the middle of the night.

What neither the Kingstons nor Harris wanted was the story splashed in the media, for that night to be talked about and analyzed and poked at by strangers. Harris had promised John Kingston that he would do whatever he could to keep the family's private struggles out of the public eye. If the news got ahold of John Kingston's story, they would undoubtedly put the pieces together, and that was something Harris couldn't afford. It would ruin everything Harris had tried to accomplish, and everything he had yet to do.

John and his family were now safely settled at a relative's house. John's wife, Catherine, and their three kids had been through enough, so Harris had fended off the media and downplayed the whole event as much as he could. Protecting them. And protecting the truth. Harris's father would have called it painting the walls to cover up the scars, but to Harris, the stakes were much higher than that.

He'd met John when he was down here for another building job last year, and had stopped in at John's barbershop for a haircut. They got to talking, and a friendship had grown between them, which was something Harris hadn't had in a long time. They'd hung out several times over the weeks Harris was supervising the building project.

John had also been there for Harris when he got the news that his mother had died—alone, because his father was off at another public event—and had been the one to drag Harris out of his room at the inn when he'd wanted to stay there and drink his days away. Harris owed John for that and for many more things that John didn't know about.

Those secrets were there for a reason, to protect other people who didn't deserve to be swept up into the McCarthy family drama again. Thankfully, it was easy for Harris to stay out of the media. Most of his work stayed under the radar, because he worked for clients with the money to keep their lives private. Every once in a while, though, his company was mentioned in the papers. Some reporters made the connection to his father, and some didn't, since McCarthy wasn't exactly an unusual last name. Either way, the less he was associated with his father, the better—the more peace he had in his life, and in his head. For too long, his father had tried to control Harris's every decision, from what time he went to bed to where he went for school, and all Harris wanted was a lot of distance between those days and now.

Except a reminder of those days had just walked back into his life.

As if on cue, the door behind him opened, and Melanie stepped onto the porch. She was wearing a pair of blue plaid flannel pants and a soft gray T-shirt that ended just above the drawstring of the pants, exposing a tiny sliver of her belly. *Nice. Very nice.*

"Couldn't sleep, either?" he said.

She jumped. "Harris. I didn't see you out here."

After he left the Comeback, he'd vowed to give Mellie space. They were done, after all, and there was no reason to keep trying to get her to spend time with him. But he was curious about her life, about her, and that was why he pointed to the second chair. "Join me. It's a gorgeous night."

"Oh, I shouldn't—"

"Hey, you can't sleep, I can't sleep. Let's have a really boring conversation and drink some chamomile tea or something."

She laughed. "Do you drink chamomile tea?"

"Hell, no. It sounds like something my grandmother

would make. I opt for the manly cure for insomnia." He hoisted his beer.

"Ah, smart move." She hesitated a moment more, then dropped into the chair beside him. "Okay, I'll stay a moment, but only because it is a nice view."

He chuckled. "I'll take that."

She turned to face him, her eyes wide and luminous. "You keep trying to act like we are friends, Harris, when last I checked, we were anything but."

"True." Their relationship had ended with an explosion. His father had told him that he'd seen Melanie with another man. Harris hadn't believed him, but then he'd driven across town, and when he pulled up outside Mellie's house, there she was, sobbing in someone else's arms. When Harris confronted her, she hadn't denied it. She'd just cried and said over and over again that it wasn't what he thought, but the embrace he'd seen said otherwise. He'd stood there, with a ring in his pocket, and seen his whole life fall apart.

Their breakup had almost destroyed him. He'd been young and in love, or so he'd thought, and even having her this close to him brought up all the feelings he had tried to bury a decade ago.

"I'm sorry about how things ended," he said. He'd been a teenage boy, quick to anger, slow to listen. He'd basically yelled at her and stomped off. Regardless of what she'd done, that moment was one he regretted. "I could have handled that better."

She waved off his words. "It doesn't matter. It's all in the past."

"Is it?"

Her gaze stopped meeting his. "We've been apart for more than ten years. We've both had relationships in that time, and I've gotten married—"

"And divorced." He wondered what kind of man would let Mellie go, then remembered he had done that very thing—after he'd seen her with another man she couldn't explain. Her cheating on him had destroyed their relationship. Maybe some relationships were just meant to end.

She got to her feet and faced the lake, her back to him. "And since then, we've both moved on, pursued other paths, other interests, other people," she said. "Whatever we had back in high school, we've long since outgrown."

He rose, shifted into place beside her. She pivoted, just a little, but didn't back away. His gaze flicked to that sliver of skin, then back to her face. Damn, she looked beautiful, even with her hair back in a ponytail and her face bare of makeup. He'd missed her, more than he'd realized until he saw her on that bar stool. Had her cheating been part of teenage immaturity, the same as his over-the-top reaction? Or something more? Had their relationship ever meant as much to her as it did to him? "Did we?"

She cut her gaze away. "Harris, this is pointless—"

He caught her chin and brought her to face him. Then just as quickly, let her go. What was he doing? "Sorry. I…I just don't want us to have hard feelings."

She gave him a short nod. "Fine. We've made amends. Now we can go to sleep with clear consciences."

If only that were true. His conscience was still

haunted by his father's actions, his mother's sorrow, the dominoes that kept falling. Harris took a sip of beer and leaned against the deck railing.

"I don't know about you, but I'm not sleepy yet." A few minutes passed, with only the chirp of the crickets and the occasional call of a lonely loon breaking the silence. "I love this time of day."

"I remember."

Did she think of those days, too? Did she remember the long walks in the woods and the afternoons by the creek, and the way a few simple words from her would turn his days around? Damn, he had loved her then. Why had she turned to someone else while still claiming to love him? Had she lied about her feelings? Or had he been too infatuated to see the truth?

"It's almost magical, you know?" When he was young, he'd sneaked out of the house at night, soaking in the freedom of the dark, the quiet, the fact that he was breaking the rules. "When I'm stuck at work, I often take a walk at night. It helps clear my head."

"I do the same thing sometimes." She leaned back against a post and toed a circle on the wooden decking. "So, why custom home building?"

He shrugged. "It was a way to combine my loves of drawing, numbers and being hands-on. The job checked all the boxes." He tipped his beer in her direction. "Why magazine writer? I thought you wanted to be a journalist."

"Well, my job is definitely not what I thought I'd end up doing." She sighed, and her gaze went to the lake. "I always wanted to write things that mattered. Stories that people cared about."

She seemed sad—lost, almost. The part of him that had never stopped caring about her—not really— wanted to reach out and hug her and make it all better. "Then why not leave the magazine and write what you really want to write? I know that takes a leap of faith— it's a leap I had to take when I quit my job. Scary as hell, but worth it in the end."

She scoffed. "Easier said than done, Harris. I can't afford to just up and do something else. Writing about the new trend in sandals for summer was a way to pay my bills."

Was. Past tense. Maybe just an accidental slip of the tongue?

He covered her hand with his own. It was the second time he'd touched her tonight, and that familiar zing ran through him again. "Then write about something that makes you excited to get out of bed in the morning. I remember how you were always carrying around that pad of paper. You loved writing, loved telling stories. I don't see that same excitement in your face now."

"Well, I'm not a naive kid now. I haven't been for a long time. You don't know me, Harris. Not anymore." She turned away and broke their connection. "I...I should probably get back to bed."

Just before she opened the door, he said, "Remember that time we went skinny-dipping in the high school pool?"

What the hell? Where did that come from?

"What made you think of that?"

He nodded at the dark expanse below the hill. He could hear Mellie laughing in that long-ago memory, see the flash of her pale skin before she dived into the water, tempting him, daring him, to loosen the shackles that hung around his life. "That lake down there. Probably still warm at this time of year."

He really was a glutton for punishment. They were over, and for good reason. What was he trying to resurrect here?

"I am not skinny-dipping with you, Harris McCarthy. Regardless of the temperature of the water."

He chuckled at the mock propriety in her voice, the feigned outrage. The Mellie he remembered would have taken almost any risk, leaped off any cliff. She'd always been so much braver than him, daring him to live outside the lines his father had painted around him from birth. It took a lot more years after they'd broken up before Harris got brave enough to tell his father no and to strike out on his own.

If he'd stayed with Mellie, would he have found the courage sooner? The consequences of staying as long as he had…well, Harris would be paying for those for a while. If their relationship had been different—had been what he'd *thought* it was—how would that have changed things for him? "We had a hell of a time that night."

"Until the janitor caught us. We almost got expelled." She shook her head, and the moment of lightness disappeared from her face. "Why are you bringing up old history?"

"Because I've never had as much fun with anyone as I have with you, Mellie. And I miss that."

She hesitated, and for a second, he hoped she would reconsider the wall she'd kept between them. "I…well, I still don't think we should—"

"Be friends? Because that's all I'm asking." He wanted to tell her that he'd had a hell of a week, and he could really use some company. Especially from the one woman who had always made him laugh. But saying that would mean opening up about what was bothering him, all the heaviness weighing him down, and there was no way Harris wanted to do that right now. Or ever.

"I just came out for a breath of fresh air. Maybe another time, Harris." Then she turned on her heel and went back into the inn.

Chapter Three

Melanie pulled open the door to the *Stone Gap Gazette* a little after nine the next morning. It was a small building, tucked at the end of a side street. The bell over the door let out a tinny ring as she went inside, and the wood floors beneath her feet creaked.

A wizened old man got to his feet when she entered. The ball cap on his head shadowed his craggy features. "Can I help you?"

She put on a bright smile and tried to quell the nerves in her gut. She'd gone on dozens of interviews in the many, many months since she'd lost her job. For weeks on end, not a single callback, not a single offer. She was beginning to wonder if she was in the wrong field all together, despite what Harris had said last night. All she had was the one maybe offer from that prestigious online magazine—which would only become a *yes* if she proved her depth as a journalist.

"Good morning." She widened her smile, then skipped the small talk. If she was going to be rejected, might as well get it over with quickly. "I heard you need some writing help for the next couple of weeks."

"I need help for a lot longer than that, but yeah, I'd love to get an experienced writer in here. I'm Saul Richardson, editor and chief bottle washer. And you are?"

"Melanie Cooper." *Unemployed writer who is hoping she doesn't strike out once again.*

They shook hands, then he peered at her over his glasses. He was only a couple inches taller than her, his back hunched from years of sitting at a desk, but his gaze was bright and clear as a laser. "Are you an experienced writer?"

She nodded. "Five years with *City Girl* magazine in New York. If you want to pull up my clips, they're all archived on the magazine's website." So many other places she'd interviewed at in New York had been unimpressed with her credentials. In a city that big, writers were a dime a dozen, especially ones with no hard journalism experience. She'd never even gotten a call after sending her résumé to the more serious publications in town, like the *Times* and the *New Yorker*. Maybe in a small town, where published writers were few and far between, she'd have a better shot.

Saul gave her one last assessment, then nodded. "I'll do that. In fact, why don't you go grab a bite to eat over at the café while I take a peek at your work. When you get back, we'll see if you have the right stuff for the *Stone Gap Gazette*. I know it might just seem like a small-town paper to other folks, but it's my baby, and I can't let just anyone work here."

Melanie chuckled. She liked Saul, with his fierce protectiveness of his paper, his caution at hiring just anyone. She could already tell he'd be a great editor to work for. He seemed passionate, but smart and fair. "I can understand that. I used to be editor of my high school newspaper, and I had pretty much the same attitude as you. So I can appreciate your commitment to quality and to maintaining the paper's reputation. I'll be back in a few minutes." She gave him the URL for the magazine's archives, then headed across the street to Mabel's Diner.

Like pretty much everything in Stone Gap, the diner was a cozy place, filled with locals on this bright Wednesday morning, and a bustling waitstaff hurrying back and forth with omelets and coffees. So unlike New York, with its hordes of people in suits flowing in a black and gray sea down the crowded streets, and the overpriced coffee shops where a simple latte cost as much as the entire Hearty Man Breakfast Platter at Mabel's.

She opted to sit at one of the two remaining free seats at the counter and ordered a coffee and a plate of scrambled eggs from the bubbly girl behind the counter. Moments later, a good-looking dark-haired man sat on the last empty stool.

"Morning," he said, giving her a friendly nod. "You must be new in town."

Melanie laughed. "Do I have that tattooed on my forehead or something? Everyone says that. And the next question is—"

"Are you staying at the Stone Gap Inn?" he finished for her. "I hope you are, because I'm Jack Barlow, son of Della, who is part owner of the inn." He thrust out his hand.

"I'm Melanie. Nice to meet you. Your mom mentioned you and your brothers when she talked about the renovations. I've heard the Barlow name mentioned around town, too, quite often." Yet another way this town differed from New York City, or even the large town where she'd grown up in Connecticut. No wonder Abby loved it here. The town perfectly suited her home-centered sister.

"That's because my brothers and I are a little notorious around town for getting into trouble." He grinned. "I hope you're enjoying your stay."

"I am. The inn is wonderful. I haven't met your mother yet, but Mavis has been really sweet and friendly." The waitress slid her coffee over, and Melanie thanked the girl. She shook in some sugar and poured in a little creamer. "I'm only here for a week or so, in town for my sister Abby's wedding."

"Abby and Dylan? Really great couple." Jack took a sip of his coffee, then waved hello to a few people who had just walked in, before swiveling his attention back to Melanie. "My wife, Meri, is the photographer."

"Really? My sister was singing her praises for helping her save the wedding when a bunch of things went wrong." She took a sip of the rich, dark coffee. "This is a small place."

Jack chuckled. "That's pretty much Stone Gap in a nutshell. Everyone knows everyone, and we all help each other out. Like Dylan—when his uncle needed him, he was here. The things Dylan has done with that community center have been fabulous. Really turned the place around, and made it so popular we have kids from out of town who want to come hang out in the afternoons."

"That's great." She took a sip of coffee, her mind shifting away from her sister's life and back to the editor waiting across the street for her to wow him. "Do you think the community center would make a good feature for the town paper? I'm interviewing over there after breakfast and would love to go back to the editor with a story idea or two."

Jack shook his head. "Saul just did a piece on the community center a month ago. And one on the inn."

"Oh. Okay." Being new in town came with a lot of disadvantages—mainly that she didn't know what had already been written about. She wondered if maybe Saul would be interested in profiles of the local businesspeople, or maybe one on the impact of the inn on the town. Okay, so those were all boring ideas, not jump-start-her-career ideas. A story about a *bona-fide hero* would land her an above-the-fold, front-page credential, but wasting that on the *Stone Gap Gazette* didn't make sense.

Jack thanked the waitress for a refill of his coffee

and took a few sips, quiet for now. Melanie ate her eggs and tried not to let her optimism fade.

"You know," Jack began, "the one story Saul hasn't covered—and not for lack of trying from what I hear—is the fire out at the Kingston place. This guy from out of town—damn, I forget his name, but he was a contractor or something, I think. Anyway, he rushed in there and saved every last member of the family."

That sure sounded like a hero story. And it had to be the one involving Harris McCarthy. He was the only out-of-town contractor she knew, and the man at the bar had said something about him being a local hero. But Harris...rushing into a burning building? Really?

Was it all that implausible? Just because he'd broken her heart and let her down when she needed him most didn't make him unheroic. Years and years ago, Harris had once carried an injured dog for three miles, over rugged terrain, to get him to a vet. That was hero material. A man didn't lose that just because he grew up—and broke a few hearts along the way.

Melanie leaned a little closer and tried not to look too eager. "I heard a little about that at the Comeback Bar last night."

"Quite the event. Partly because this town is so small, just about anything becomes news." Jack chuckled. "Anyway, it's got the town all abuzz. Normally something like that happens, the family gets news coverage and folks are lining up to drop off clothes and food, but this time, the Kingstons are staying mum. Damnedest thing."

In Melanie's experience, people who kept quiet had

something to hide. Which had all the earmarks of a career-rejuvenating article. The kind of story that made her want to race to her keyboard in the morning, the kind of story she'd dreamed of writing the day she arrived in New York. Maybe if she wrote this story, she could trace her way back to the life she'd been seeking all this time and never quite found.

Melanie dropped some bills on the counter and took a quick gulp of coffee. The urge to get the interviews, write the words, land the job, rushed through her. The drive she'd lost long ago sprang to life. "Thanks for the tip, Jack."

"You're welcome. Anytime. Welcome to Stone Gap, by the way."

She smiled. "Thanks. It's a great town. I don't know what I expected, but it seems so…cozy. Like a cabin in the woods or some cliché like that."

"Be careful," Jack said. "Stone Gap is the kind of town that grows on you. Before you know it, you're buying a sofa and planting hydrangeas."

Melanie laughed. "I'm not the hydrangea-planting kind of person. And Stone Gap is just a temporary stop." *I'm only staying long enough to get my life back on track.*

And now, with the chance to nab an exclusive story, that path felt closer than ever.

Chapter Four

An hour later, Melanie had a job at the *Stone Gap Gazette*, an assignment to interview Stone Gap's oldest living resident and a plan. The sense of failure that had plagued her since her divorce and losing her job began to lift.

The position she'd gotten wasn't the job she needed, or a job that would turn her life around, but it was a step in the right direction. Plus, with some more serious clips on her résumé, she could drag herself out of the land of waterproof mascara options and into a career with meat. A career that made her feel like she was using her writing powers for good, not for evil white lies.

Except this job came at a price she wasn't sure she could pay, despite her earlier confidence in the diner.

The job interview had gone well at first, with Saul complimenting her work at *City Girl*. "It isn't the kind of thing we run in the paper here, of course." He chuckled. "This town isn't exactly big into the latest trends in platform heels. But you have a nice writing style. I really liked that piece you did on those college grads who moved to New York. That whole 'first year in the city' story was really well done."

She blushed. It was the one set of articles at *City Girl* that had kept her there, thinking maybe the series would do so well that the magazine would commission more stories like that from her. Instead, a new editor had come in, and the magazine had shifted even further away from anything with depth. When Melanie had complained about the lack of scope and the inanity of most of what she wrote, the new senior editor had simply said, "Perhaps it's best if we part ways."

Just like that, Melanie was out of a job. She'd come home that day, hoping Adam would finally step out of his self-absorbed self and offer her some comfort, or at the very least a glass of wine and some dinner. But Adam hadn't been there. Not that day, not that night. Not for the entire year before, heck, not for most of their marriage. Adam had turned out to be a self-centered man who did what pleased him, and who had sucked Melanie in with an irresistible charm and an almost pouty *I need you* attitude when she'd met him.

The day she'd lost her job, Adam came home late the next morning, and before she could confront him or tell him about her job, he'd told her he was in love with Cheri of the heart-dotted letters. *She gets me,* he'd said. *She gets what's important to me. You're way too serious, Melanie.*

She'd scraped by through their quickie divorce and the year since on some freelance work, her savings and the small settlement with Adam, but by this point, she was near the end of her rope. She sat across from Saul in a room that still smelled like ink and paper, even though the *Stone Gap Gazette* had long ago switched to digital printing, and felt that first sense of light at the end of the tunnel.

"I heard there was a fire and a family got rescued," Melanie said. "I was thinking that might—"

"I've been trying six ways to Sunday to get an interview on that one and haven't been able to. For now, how about you get your feet wet, show me what you can do? I'll start you off with a piece on Evelyn Ross She's our oldest living resident, celebrating her hundred and second birthday this Tuesday. If you can get me that by Friday morning, I can put it in the next edition." He slid a piece of paper with Evelyn's contact info across the desk. "Eight hundred words, with all those tips on living longer. I'll pay you by the piece, a hundred dollars. It's not much, but it's something."

"Can do. Thank you, Mr. Richardson."

"Call me Saul. Nobody ever calls me Mister anything unless they're trying to sell me something. I'm not much for formality, anyway." He chuckled again.

Melanie got to her feet. All those interviews, all those résumés sent out, and finally—*finally*—she had a job—well, okay, a few pieces to write. Once she used these more serious clips and her restored confidence to springboard back into a career in New York, she could tell Abby the truth about what had happened in the last year. They'd have a good laugh, and Abby would see she didn't have to worry so much about her little sister. "Thank you again, Saul. I appreciate the assignment." She started to turn away.

"You know, I was thinking…"

She turned back. "Yes?"

"About what you said earlier. Maybe you *could* do that story on the fire. You're new in town, determined to get the story…maybe you can sweet-talk your way into finding out what happened over at the Kingston house the other night. Lord knows I've tried, but those folks see me coming and lock their door twice. Whole damned town is talking about it, except the family and that guy who rescued them. Harry? Harvey?"

"Harris."

Saul arched a brow. "Do you know him? That contractor fellow?"

"A…a little." *As in I used to be in love with him, and when he smiles at me, I lose my concentration. Yeah, just a little.*

"You get that story, and you'll be the envy of all the papers in a five-county area. Hell, *I'll* be the envy of all those papers, and I'll get a much-needed boost in subscriptions if they see that this little paper is doing big things. Editors love that feel-good, happy-ending stuff. It's the kind of scoop that can get you hired at the *Charlotte Observer*." He gave her a long, assessing glance. "Because I get the feeling you aren't much for small-town life."

"Well, I…" She didn't know what to say. If she admitted she saw these assignments as a stepping-stone, then Saul would undoubtedly rescind his offer of work, and that would ruin everything. Her reboot would be dead before it got off the ground.

"It's okay." He gave her a soft smile. "I once dreamed of bigger things, too. Until I fell in love and settled in this sleepy little town for good. Stone Gap has been good to me, so I have no regrets."

Melanie just smiled.

"Anyway, I'm glad to have the help, even if it's only for now. God will take care of the rest when it comes time."

She wasn't sure about the heaven-sent help, but she kept that to herself. "Thank you for the job. You can count on me, Saul."

Except as she walked down Main Street, she wasn't so sure Saul had put all his eggs in the right basket. A profile on the oldest living resident would be a piece of cake. Getting close enough to Harris again to get him to open up about what was clearly a sore subject—

Not easy at all. Mainly because getting close to Harris came with a whole other list of problems. Already, images of him danced around the edges of her thoughts. The memory of him touching her, the yearning need she'd felt last night, thinking of how good he kissed, how much she'd missed those touches, all of that hanging on the edges of the pain from years ago.

Yeah, not easy at all.

Melanie ducked into Betty's Bakery, a quaint little shop nestled between George's Deli and a small patch of land converted into a playground to honor a fallen hometown soldier. At the bottom of the sign for the park, she saw the words *Built by Jack Barlow*. She wasn't surprised. The man she had met earlier clearly cared about this town and seemed the type to give back with something like this. Maybe that was the kind of thing that kept the town talking about the Barlows, rather than whatever things they'd gotten into trouble for when they were boys. It was another of those small-town touches that made Melanie feel like she was ten million miles away from New York.

Abby was sitting alone at a small white wrought iron café table inside the bakery, with a set of plates and silverware beside her. "You're here! I was getting worried." Abby shifted her purse to the floor to make room for Melanie to sit beside her.

"Sorry. I was meeting with the editor of the paper. I picked up an assignment for while I'm here."

"You did? That's great. But…you're so busy already with the magazine. Are you sure you can take on the extra work?" Abby touched her sister's cheek. "You work so hard, and I worry about you."

Melanie covered Abby's hand with her own. If only Abby knew how little Melanie had actually worked in the last year. "You have enough to worry about for the next couple of weeks—heck, all the time. The wedding, Ma, your kids, your job. Just let me worry about me, okay?"

Pink and white shantung draped the walls of the cake-tasting room. Rhinestones beaded the edges, circled the tables, encrusted faux tiaras at the place settings. The place was less bakery and more bridal suite on steroids. "Speaking of which, where is Ma? I thought she was coming, too."

The door to the shop opened just then, and their mother strode in. "Goodness, do we ever get a break from the heat here?"

Melanie opted not to have the heat argument again, especially given the temperature outside was in the low seventies. Instead, she pulled out a chair between her and Abby. "Cake will make everything better."

"Only if it's good cake," Cynthia said, not so sotto voce. "I've been to some bakeries where I swear they learned to bake at a fast food restaurant. Just horrible."

"This is a great bakery, Ma," Abby said. "I've met the owners. They're lovely people."

"We'll see. Considering what they charge, they'd better be."

Abby and Melanie exchanged a look. Hope warred with frustration on Abby's face. Melanie crossed her fingers under the table. Maybe Ma would love the cake so much she wouldn't stop eating to complain and criticize.

And maybe the moon would suddenly turn to gold, too.

A buxom woman with gray hair in a tight bun bustled out of the kitchen, balancing cake samples and some napkins. "Hello, Abby and family! You must be the mother of the bride and the lovely maid of honor I've heard so much about." She put down the plates and shook with Cynthia, then Melanie. "I'm Betty, the owner of this bakery, and the wife of the one next door."

Melanie laughed. That was kind of cute, husband and wife owning businesses right beside each other. That way they were together, but not *together*. She couldn't imagine being connected with someone like that. Part of what had kept her and Adam together as long as they were was the fact that they were rarely in the same space. He traveled often, and that meant every visit home became a honeymoon. It wasn't until he was in town for several months that she realized they had almost nothing in common. He'd been so charming when they dated, and the fraction of time they'd spent together between his assignments had been romantic and short. Probably because anything more than a week together would have opened her eyes to his real personality.

She turned her attention back to something that rarely disappointed—dessert. The cake samples filled the small table. White cake, chocolate cake, buttery pound cake. Melanie pressed a hand to her stomach. "Oh my God. Every slice looks amazing."

"I think this might be my favorite part of wedding planning." Abby picked up a fork and aimed for the first slice. Betty explained it was a vanilla sponge with a raspberry center, which Abby dug into, while Melanie opted to try the chocolate cake with layers of caramel.

They rotated the plates, trying a bite of each. Ma took small bites, without commenting. Betty filled the awkward silence with wedding disaster stories, including one where a bride accidentally fell in the hotel pool on her march down the temporary aisle bridge. Soon Abby and Melanie were laughing, and the tension with their mother had disappeared. Almost.

Melanie couldn't help but feel sorry for Abby. She could see the disappointment in her sister's face every time she glanced at Ma. Abby had undoubtedly dreamed that their mother would be enthusiastically involved, but history had already dictated the opposite. Ma hadn't been hands-on with Abby's first wedding and had complained that it was too far to go to New York to help with Melanie's. And throughout their lives, even when she'd been there for important events, she'd never seemed proud or excited. Why would either of them expect anything different from her now?

Abby narrowed her cake choices down to the raspberry-filled one and a peanut butter cake drizzled with chocolate ganache. "I can't choose. I love them both."

"Then maybe have each tier a different flavor?" Melanie said. "That way, we get the best of both worlds. It's your wedding. Do it up big—in cake, at least."

"That's a great idea. I can do two different tiers, easily, the raspberry on one and chocolate on the other." Betty began writing up the order. Melanie stacked the empty plates—they'd done more than tasted; they'd eaten every last bite.

"An awful lot of expense to have two different flavors. Like that monstrosity you had at your wedding. Half went uneaten. Such a waste," Ma said. "Melanie, tell her."

Okay, so maybe the cake at her wedding to Adam had been over-the-top and one of many extravagant purchases that day that Ma had criticized. Long after the bills were paid, Melanie had realized the overdone

flowers and towering dessert had been her focus in the
weeks leading up to the wedding—instead of the mistake she was making in marrying Adam. Her sister,
however, wasn't making a mistake. Dylan clearly loved
her, loved the boys and was an all-around great guy. If
Abby wanted a ten-tier cake with dancing marionettes,
that was fine with Melanie.

"It's Abby's wedding. I think she should do what
she wants." As Melanie handed the empty plates to the
shop owner, Abby grabbed her sister's hand.

"Mel, where's your wedding ring?"

Melanie froze. She had forgotten all about her ring.
The day Adam left her, she'd put it in her jewelry box
and hadn't taken it out until last month—when she'd sold
it to help pay the bills. The alimony she'd been awarded
had been minimal, mainly because they'd been married
such a short time and Adam was supposedly "still struggling" in his career. Plus, she'd had a job when she got
divorced, all part of the alimony equation. Now she had
no job, no ring, no savings. "Uh, I forgot it at home."

Abby's brow furrowed. "Are things okay between
you and Adam?"

Here was Melanie's opportunity to come clean. To
say, *actually, nothing is okay right now.* She started
to open her mouth, but her mother interrupted first.

"Of course they are," Ma said. "Melanie is *finally*
settled down with a handsome, employed young man.
Took her long enough to figure out her life, I might add.
I'm glad that both of you girls have your lives on track."

And she gave Melanie a smile. The first genuine
smile Melanie had seen since she arrived. The little

girl in Melanie who'd been seeking approval from the day she was born just nodded and agreed.

Chicken.

Harris tucked the rebuilding plans into the pocket of his jacket, thanked the building inspector, then headed out to Main Street. He'd hired a truck and a few men with strong backs, then spent the morning out at the Kingston house, assessing the damage and making a plan for demolition and rebuilding. Nearly everything had been lost to the flames, but the material things could be replaced. Harris had already set up a fund at the Stone Gap bank, because people wanted to help. He was also working on finding the family a rental house near the school system so they could move out of their cramped relative's home. In the meantime, the plans for rebuilding were nearly approved. A couple more days and the planning commission would meet, and hopefully everything would go off without a hitch.

Harris was more concerned about John's state of mind. He'd tried to call the other man several times, but more often than not, the calls went to voice mail. He'd kept to himself yesterday, quiet and depressed. Harris knew John blamed himself for the fire, but Harris also knew John was placing the blame in the wrong place.

Harris checked his cell phone. No return text or calls from John. He placed another one, but once again, the call went straight to voice mail.

Guilt pressed on his chest. He should have paid closer attention to his friend in the days before the fire. Or answered the phone when John had called earlier that night. Harris had made the mistake of thinking all was well, then John had been hit by one more blow, and the delicate edge he'd been teetering on had broken.

Harris sighed and tucked the phone away. Maybe John just needed a little time to process what had happened. Or maybe it was better if Harris stayed away before his father got wind of what he was up to.

For years, Harris had been trying to right the wrongs of the past, undo at least some of the damage done by his father's ruthless business decisions. Pay the penance for mistakes he had made. But the list was long, and at some point, someone was going to put the pieces together, and Harris's efforts to try to heal the wounds of the past would be discovered.

Deep down inside, he knew these decisions hadn't been his. But he had been the executioner, and that meant a large percentage of the responsibility fell on his shoulders. His father would never make it right, but Harris would, the best he could.

And still it wasn't enough. Never enough to lift that horsehair shirt of guilt.

Just then the door to Betty's Bakery opened, and Melanie stepped outside. She had her dark hair down and wavy today, the long tresses skating over her shoulders, tickling the small of her back. She was wearing jeans and little black boots that added a few inches to her height. Her plain white T-shirt was offset by a caramel leather jacket that had been well worn and loved. She looked sexy and dangerous, all at once.

He thought of that late night on the back deck of the inn. How close he'd come to kissing her. How much he still wanted to. It was as if a part of him kept forgetting her cheating on him, the pain of that betrayal, how much it hurt him in the weeks after they broke up.

What would happen now if they tried again, as adults? Without the immaturity they'd had when they were eighteen? Would their relationship be more nuanced? Richer? Stronger? Or was he just caught in some reminiscent time warp?

Was he really that desperate to see if her touch would still ease his soul, as it had all those years ago? Back then, being with Mellie had been the only place where Harris could forget his life for a moment. Forget who his father was. Forget the expectations that waited for him. Forget the detritus that followed him like a stubborn shadow.

Instead of turning toward him, Mellie went left and into the park. Harris had spent more than one afternoon in the Eli Delacorte Memorial Park, a beautiful space that Jack Barlow had erected as a memorial to a friend he'd lost in the war. It was a weekday and older kids were in school. Only a few moms of toddlers lingered by a bench at the back of the park. The bright blue playground equipment meant for bigger kids was empty. Melanie dropped onto a large gray-and-red metal circle, leaning against one of the striped handles that kids held on to when the wheel spun. She put her head into her hands, and his heart caught.

"Hey, you okay?"

She jumped at the sound of his voice. "Do you always go around in stealth mode? That's like the third time you've surprised me."

"Sorry." He settled into the space beside her, their bodies separated by the slim curved handle. The circle pivoted a little with the addition of his weight. "You looked upset. You okay?"

She shrugged. "Just dealing with my mom. Or more to the point, watching Abby deal with our mom's constant criticism. Nothing is ever good enough. And the things that are…"

Her voice trailed off, something clearly left unsaid. Mellie's mother had always been judgmental and hard on her, something Harris knew all too well with his own father. "You want to talk about it?" he asked.

What was he doing? This was the woman who broke his heart. The woman he had once wanted to marry, before he'd seen her with someone else. The woman whom he swore he would never get close to again because what they had was done and over. They'd caught up last night, and he had vowed to draw the line there. And yet here he was, sitting a few inches away, trying not to give her a hug. *Masochist.*

"Talking about it never changed anything." She got to her feet, brushed imaginary dirt off her jeans, then crossed to the slide and leaned against the ladder stairs.

He went with her and stood on the other side of the ladder, their backs against the cool coated metal railing. Silence filled the space between them, peppered with the occasional call of a bird or soft whoosh of a passing car. If Mellie didn't want to talk about what was bothering her, Harris was the last person to push her to do otherwise. He had plenty of stuff in his own life that he kept swept under the rug. Most notably, a history with his father that he didn't want anyone to know about, because of the part he had played.

Suddenly, she shoved off from the railing and moved in front of him. "You asked me out the other night. Does that offer still stand?"

He blinked. He should say no. Should stay away. But he didn't. "Uh, yeah. Of course. What made you change your mind?"

"I'm a woman. I'm allowed to do that." She gave him a grin, but it seemed to flicker and he wondered if there was something else beneath her words. "It'd be nice to catch up, Harris."

He thought they'd already done that in the bar and on the porch last night, but he didn't question her. Mellie was smiling, and that smile did something to his common sense.

Maybe her night had been just as distracted with thoughts of him. Or maybe she'd felt that same tension on the deck that he had. He took a step forward, which brought them within inches of each other. Her perfume curled into the space, a lure drawing him even closer. "Catch up?"

"Yes," she said, but the word was almost a breath. Her eyes caught his, held. "I'd love to hear all about what you've been up to since…"

"Since we broke up," he finished, as if saying the words erased it all. "That was a long time ago. Water under the bridge."

But was it? Seemed to him, given the riot in his gut, that the water was still a bit turbulent. Maybe because he still had questions that had never been answered.

"Good." She smiled again. "Then that means we can be friends."

The single word punched him in the gut. "Friends? Is that what we are?"

Why did he care? She'd broken his heart, ruined his life that summer. He didn't need her back in his life as some do-over relationship or some hokey second-chance love. He had other things to concentrate on right now, far more important things.

"What else could we be?" Mellie said. "I'm here for the wedding, then I'm going back to New York."

Exactly. Just friends. Anything more would be... complicated. After these couple of weeks, maybe they would stay in touch by email or something.

"Exactly," he echoed. He was having a little trouble coming up with words of his own. Maybe it was her perfume—something darker and spicier than she'd worn years ago. Or maybe it was her curves, more tempting now than ever. Or maybe it was the way she kept looking at him as if nothing had happened that summer night.

A girl like that will ruin you, Harris. All she does is distract you from your goals. So be smart and walk away before she traps you into marriage with a bunch of kids.

His father had never liked Melanie and told Harris often that he could do better. In Phillip's mind, Harris was going to marry some equally driven type-A. A lawyer or doctor or something who would fit with his father's image of what their family should be. But Harris had been in love with freewheeling, adventurous, saucy Melanie Cooper.

But all that was years in the past, and Harris no longer lived under the same roof as Phillip McCarthy. What Harris did with his life, and his love life, wasn't his father's concern anymore. Nor was something that had happened a decade ago.

"Just friends is good, right?" Mellie said, but her sentence ended with a lilt of doubt. "Because..."

"All the rest is in the past." He moved closer and traced along her jaw, ran his thumb over her lips. They parted and she inhaled, her eyes wide. He shifted closer still, entranced, and for that moment, he was eighteen again, and she was the most beautiful thing he'd ever seen. "Right?"

"Right," she said, but the word trailed off halfway through, and she turned her cheek to his hand and closed her eyes.

Harris leaned in and kissed her. Mellie melted into him by degrees, her body sliding closer and closer, until he couldn't tell where he ended and she began. His arms went around her back and she opened to him, tangling her fingers in his hair, returning his kiss move for move.

Nothing had died between them, he realized. Not a single damned thing. He wasn't sure if that was a good thing or a very, very dangerous one. Either way, Harris wasn't about to start asking questions now.

Chapter Five

For a solid minute, Melanie was seventeen again and caught in the shadows of the high school bleachers while Harris kissed her and turned her world upside down. There'd always been something about his touch, something almost…magical that made all rational thought disappear.

Even now, almost a decade later, he had that effect on her, damn it. She wasn't here to kiss him or fall for him or anything stupid like that. She was here for a shot at a career-making story—a means to a new end that was far from Stone Gap and Harris McCarthy.

She reminded herself that when she had needed him most, years ago, Harris had betrayed her. He had jumped to conclusions and broken up with her, unwilling to hear her side or to give her even a shadow of a doubt. He'd turned into someone she didn't recognize.

Her real reason for asking him to go out was to get the inside scoop on the fire. Harris would open up, she'd have her article and her career would be reawakened, all without falling for him again. It was the least he owed her, after breaking her heart and leaving her alone on her darkest day. Except somehow she had ended up kissing him just now. What was that about?

Working toward a new job—0. Getting involved in a mess—1.

She put her hands between them—damn, when did his chest get so much more solid and muscular?—and pushed hard, stepping back as she did and colliding with the ladder. The jarring impact was a relief—it cleared her head before she caved to more than just a kiss. "What was that?"

He grinned. "A kiss. Unless it's been so long you've forgotten what it's like to be kissed by me?"

She definitely hadn't forgotten that. She'd been thinking about that very thing way too much since she ran into Harris in the bar. "That wasn't part of catching up."

"I'm sorry. I must have misread you," Harris said.

He hadn't misread her, not one bit. In fact, every single nerve and hormone in her body had been leaning toward Harris, begging for a kiss. The logical side of her brain, however, was the party pooper that had reminded her that she was here for a job, not a one-night stand with a man she'd never truly forgotten. Yet another reason to keep this light and breezy and focus on the story, not on the man. "Either way, I think it's best if we keep things…uncomplicated."

"As you wish."

The one line from *The Princess Bride*, a favorite movie for both of them, echoed in the air, reminding her of the connection she'd once shared with Harris. One time, Melanie had sat down with Adam on a lazy Sunday morning and turned on the classic fairy tale. Within five minutes, Adam had been bored and switched the channel to golf. Melanie couldn't help but compare the two men, then and now. With Harris, things had always been easy, natural. With Adam, she'd constantly felt like she was trying to make the pieces of him fit with her.

Why did Harris have to go and break her heart, anyway? She'd been so in love with him back then, so convinced they were forever, and then he'd broken it off, accusing her without hearing her side, and left her stunned and crying. *Stupid boy*, she thought, the same thing she and Abby used to whisper late at night when they were trying to figure out the hidden meaning behind a boy's glance or smile or note.

Harris's breakup had taken her years to forget. It hadn't been a blind date standing her up or a man who didn't call after a few nice dates. It had been Harris, and when it had happened, he had been her everything. And from that day forward, when Melanie realized the adult consequences of adult decisions, she had stopped living life by the seat of her pants and took the safe route of a job, a marriage that didn't fulfill her, and a life insurance policy. No more risks, no more bad choices.

"How about we take a grand tour of Stone Gap?" Harris asked, dragging her attention back to him, to the present. "I'm sure your sister is crazy busy with wedding plans, and it'd be a shame to miss out on the quaintness of this place. So I'm offering, as your *friend*, to be your tour guide. For a strictly platonic date."

"Sure." Though, put that way, with the words *platonic* and *friend*, the whole thing sounded kind of… sad. Then again, her reasons for agreeing to the grand tour weren't exactly about being friends, more of a means to an end—her own end. Was it wrong that she was reconnecting with Harris just to get him to talk to her for the paper?

Then why hadn't she mentioned it? Why take this circuitous route to what she wanted?

She pushed the doubts away. It wasn't as if she was doing anything bad. She wanted to write a story that would show Harris as a hero—surely he couldn't object to that. After she turned the story in, they could have a drink and laugh about what had brought them back together. As friends. Platonic friends.

Except there was that pesky matter of still being attracted to the man. Enjoying that kiss. Wondering if he would do it again. And reminding her why she had vowed to keep all that in the past.

"I've got a couple errands to run," Harris said. "How about I meet you back at the inn at five, and we start our tour of this fine town?"

"Sounds good."

"And should I presume that you definitely aren't interested in any more kisses?" He waved between them, as she had. "Because for a minute there, you seemed to be quite interested."

"You caught me off guard, that's all. I need to… prepare myself." *Liar, liar.*

He chuckled. "What am I? A history test?"

"You, Harris McCarthy, are…complicated." A family came into the park—mom, dad, baby in a stroller and a four-year-old boy barreling toward the swings. Melanie spied her mother and Abby on the sidewalk, talking. Or rather, Abby was standing stiff and resolute, while Ma wagged a finger and made some kind of judgment. Apparently the sugar rush had worn off and Ma was taking the opportunity to let loose yet another lecture. "I gotta go."

Melanie spun on her heel and hurried away before Harris could kiss her again or add yet another layer of trouble she didn't need. Or worse, before she gave in to the incessant craving in her gut to make a move on him.

Melanie plowed forward and out of the park. She didn't look back, didn't worry what Harris would think. Her emotions were all in a jumble, tangled in some weird vortex between the past and the present.

She caught up to Abby just as her sister peeled off from Ma, and Ma headed into a dress shop. "What happened?" she said to Abby.

Her sister sighed. "The usual. I don't even know why Ma came out for the wedding. She told me she's too busy to be involved in the planning."

"Too busy? Doing what? She's retired."

"Apparently she joined a book club and she's behind on reading. Oh, and there's the blanket she promised to knit for someone's grandson." Abby threw up her hands. "I can't do anything right."

"You? You always do everything right, Abs."

"No, that's you." Abby shook her head. "I know I shouldn't take it personally, but when Ma starts in on how perfect your life is… I'm sorry. It shouldn't bug me."

Melanie swallowed a lump of guilt. Maybe now was a good time to tell Abby the truth. *My life sucks. It's a train wreck.*

Abby drew her younger sister into a hug. Melanie drew a deep breath, opened her mouth… And she couldn't say the words. Yet again.

"I'm so glad you're here, Mel. Ma is driving me nuts, and with the kids and the wedding… I'm just glad to have you to lean on." Abby drew back and smiled. "Kinda ironic, huh? Me leaning on you?"

"Well, I'm not five anymore, so I think it's allowed." Melanie grinned. But inside, she was thinking what a low-life move it was to let her sister keep on thinking that Melanie could be any sort of foundation for anyone right now. *Stupid girl.*

Harris changed his shirt three times before finally settling on a blue cotton button-down. He rolled up the cuffs, threw on a pair of jeans, then headed downstairs. The B&B was definitely an unusual place to meet a date. But then again, Mellie was no ordinary woman, and this was no ordinary date.

Or rather, a not-date. It was two friends, hanging out. Nothing more, no matter how strange that seemed.

Maybe it was because he'd never really looked at Mellie that way. When he'd been young and foolish, he'd considered forever with her. Then she'd broken his heart, and he'd ended it in that kind of hurried, angry way kids did.

Now, with a lot of years between them and several more relationships, Harris understood that relationships were complicated. *All* relationships—whether they were romantic or not. He'd learned that firsthand working for his father and had grown up more in that year than in the twenty-two years before he went to work at the firm. Maybe there'd been more to that summer with Mellie than he knew. And maybe he'd been too damned young to consider forever with anyone.

He'd come close once, with his engagement to Sandra, but at the last minute he'd backed out, with some foolish idea that he could find some kind of storybook love. His father had reminded him a hundred times that waiting for some idealized version of a woman was a futile exercise. That marriages should be made between equals who brought complementary talents and backgrounds into the mix. Like a business merger, only with sex.

Harris wanted something in between the two. Something more than the cordial partnership his parents had or the fiery, intoxicating and foolish romance he'd had with Mellie.

He leaned against the archway of the dining room. The elegant wooden staircase, with its dark oak treads and white turned spindles, curved away from him and toward the second floor. At any moment, Mellie would descend, reminiscent of Scarlett O'Hara. And the rush of desire he kept telling himself didn't exist anymore would come roaring back.

What was he doing here? Chasing a memory? Hoping for some kind of closure?

His phone rang, and he fished it out of his front pocket. John Kingston's face lit up the screen. Guilt squeezed Harris's chest. If only...

But the time for if-onlys and what-ifs had already passed. What was done was done, and all Harris could do was try to make it right again.

"John. How are you, buddy? How's the family?"

"Hanging in there." John paused for a long moment. Harris had liked the man from the minute he met him. There was a reason Harris had gone to John's barber shop, when there was another much closer to the job site. Because every city Harris visited, every town he worked in, he searched for the names on his list. John's had popped up in Stone Gap. Between the clippers and the shave oil, he'd connected with John. This friendship was real, though, which was different from before. Even after Harris left town last year, they'd kept in touch via emails and texts. He liked John, liked him a lot.

"I...I realize I screwed up that night." John sighed. "I gotta get my act together or I'm going to lose everything. It's just been so hard, you know? Since my company got shut down seven years ago, it seems like nothing has gone right."

We're going to close their doors, Harris. These business owners carry too much flab in their workforce. They need to be leaner, meaner, more profitable.

That had been his father's motto for everything: *Leaner, meaner, more profitable.* Phillip McCarthy had worked his way up from being just a CPA to becoming an outside expert, flown in by struggling companies to find and eliminate the "flab." That all sounded very admirable…until a closer examination showed that Phillip "helped" companies by covertly ruining their competitors, making their problems go away. Problems like John Kingston, who had started his machining company in his basement twenty years ago, and built it to a workforce of forty dedicated people. John's company, the main supplier to a local automotive manufacturing plant, had been in the way of a much bigger, much more profitable alliance between the automotive company and a competitor's machining business. The owner of that other business had been one of Phillip McCarthy's clients—and he had offered a substantial payment to Phillip for convincing the automotive company to switch suppliers.

Over seven years ago, Harris had sat in an office hundreds of miles away, two days before Christmas, trying to get the stomach to carry out his father's instructions—and shut down Kingston Machining by yanking away the one contract that made up ninety-five percent of their business. Knowing that doing that would cripple John's company, result in the immediate layoffs of more than three dozen people, leaving them with no severance, no Christmas bonus. Harris had sat in that office for hours, staring at the photos on the website from the last three years of Kingston Machining's annual company picnics, and seen the workers and their families eating burgers and trading laughs. Happy families.

At the end of the day, he'd done what his father was paying him to do and placed the call to John's CFO, telling them their millions of dollars in potential future orders to make engine parts for the new line of pickup trucks was gone, handed off to their competitor. The man had cried on the phone, begged Harris to give the company a chance to lower their prices, become more competitive. But the decision was made, a backroom alliance made by Phillip that made a lot of wealthy people wealthier and destroyed a man's life work. The loss of the contract had gutted the company, and it had shut its doors for good three months later.

John Kingston and his forty employees had been one of the casualties in Harris's father's decisions—and Harris's own actions. So had Shawn Babcock and Georgia Thompson, who had owned a steel import company that also lost its contract with the same automotive plant. Kevin Simmons worked at the first company Harris had eviscerated when he started working for his father, a small store in the way of a major expansion Phillip had handled for one of his clients.

After Harris had left his father's firm, he'd begun to search for the people who had lost their jobs because of Phillip McCarthy's focus on profit and loss over people. Many of them had found other jobs, but many were still struggling, out of work for so long their homes were in foreclosure or already gone. Every time, Harris had come in with a "gift" and some manufactured reason why they were receiving a home, or having their current home's mortgage settled, with the taxes paid and built-in breathing room. Three families were now back on their feet, unaware of why they'd been helped or who had been their benefactor. And soon, hopefully a fourth.

He could help a hundred families, try a thousand times to repay them for his father's heartless shock-and-awe techniques, but he suspected it would never be enough. All he could do was ensure people who had been harmed had a home, a place where they felt safe. A place that would never be taken away.

"I'm trying," John said. "I really am. But losing the house…damn. How will Catherine and the kids ever forgive me when I can't forgive myself?"

"You've been through a lot. It's not all your fault." Those were the words Harris had told himself when he made the call to John's CFO that day. Harris almost admitted the truth to John now, but he stopped. The hatred John had toward Harris's father was palpable—and justified. If he knew Harris had befriended him as a way to atone for the past, John's pride would make him reject all the help Harris was trying to give him and his family.

"Yeah, Harris, it is. Or at least mostly my fault. If that selfish bastard Phillip hadn't talked the plant into shifting all their orders to the other plant, I wouldn't have had to fire everyone…" John cursed under his breath. "Doesn't matter. What's done is done, and I have to stop making mistakes because of what that man did to my livelihood. I've been going to meetings, and I'm back to counseling with Catherine. But it's still hard."

No matter how much money Harris poured into restoring lives, it didn't repair the emotional damage, the mental wounds. "Soon, it will all be much better. Reconstruction of the house will start as soon as the town approves the plans I submitted. And the build will come in under the estimate, which will make your mortgage much lower." Or zero, as Harris intended, by making up some story about the fund at the bank exceeding the amount owed on the loan. John had been on the verge of eviction when the house burned down. Harris wouldn't let that happen again.

"I can't thank you enough, Harris. I don't know why you're being so gracious to me and my family, but we sure are grateful."

"Just one friend helping another." *Liar.*

"Well, I've never had a friend like this. Like I said, I'm grateful. Me and Catherine."

Guilt filled Harris. If John only knew...

"I, uh, gotta go. Another call. Talk to you later, John," Harris said. He hung up the phone and tucked it in his pocket. The slim cell seemed to weigh ten tons. Maybe he could stop by the city planner's office tomorrow. Speed things up. Once that house was built and the Kingstons were back on their feet, Harris could leave Stone Gap and move on to another paying project while he searched for the next name on his list. And maybe this time the guilt wouldn't chase him when he left.

Della Barlow stepped into the hall, carrying a light jacket and her purse. "Harris. How are you?"

"Very well, thank you, Ms. Barlow."

She waved that off. "Everyone around here calls me Della."

The auburn-headed owner of the inn had been more than friendly to Harris both times he'd been here— she'd welcomed him like family. He half dreaded heading back to his apartment in Connecticut. Staying with Della and Mavis in this renovated home seemed a lot like walking into some Disney version of family life.

Once upon a time, Harris had imagined that life. Then he and Mellie broke up, and he'd gone to college, then to work for his father. Something inside him had been broken, and he'd allowed that to make him think being part of his father's company was the right way to fix it. He'd found out too late that all he'd done was make the broken parts worse.

"I'm heading home for the night," Della said, "but I wanted to tell you that I'll be at the Kingston house tomorrow, helping the boys and you. I can't be there all day, but I can certainly give a couple hours to such a good cause. It was so sweet of you to organize a cleanup effort." Della shook her head. "Such a tragedy. I'm so grateful no one got hurt."

"Me, too. And thank you, for the help. Your sons have done so much already." The minute the sirens sounded on the fire truck, the Barlow boys, volunteer firemen who joined after their brother Colton had been hired by the Stone Gap Fire Department, had been there, helping the fire department put out the flames, then helping the family recover their belongings.

"They love this town, and everyone in it. Everyone feels so helpless when something bad happens to good people. Helping the Kingstons get their home rebuilt is the least we can do." She put a hand on his arm and gave him a smile. "And it's really nice of you to spearhead this entire thing. You're not even a resident, and here you are, taking care of one of our own."

Harris cut his gaze away. "John deserves it. He's a great guy."

Della's smile widened. "And that's exactly why Stone Gap loves you so. You're helping a friend who so greatly needs a hand. See you tomorrow, Harris."

That wave of guilt flooded Harris, heated his face. Yes. The sooner the Kingston home was rebuilt, the better. Ever since the day he'd closed the deal that led to the firing of all those people, Harris had walked around with a sick feeling in the pit of his stomach. For a moment, he'd danced on the dark side, trying to earn the praise of a man who had none to give.

Mellie appeared at the top of the stairs, a ray of light that dragged Harris out of his dark mood. Like him, she'd opted for something a step above casual, with a silky red shirt that hung loose over a pair of black skinny jeans. She had her hair back with a clip, leaving a couple of tendrils curling along her neck. His breath caught for a second.

What was that thing about just being friends?

"You look beautiful," he said as she descended and closed the gap between them.

"Thank you." She shot him a teasing grin. "You don't look so bad yourself."

He chuckled. "You really know the way to flatter a man." Some vain part of him wondered if she was still attracted to him. She had, after all, pushed him away after their kiss earlier. Message clear: *Not interested in you that way. Not anymore.*

But she was here tonight, and even if the whole thing was as platonic as a bologna sandwich, he was going to enjoy the moment. He fell into step beside her, and the two of them crossed to the front door. He opened it and waited for her to pass first.

"My, my Harris." Mellie arched a brow. "Are you a gentleman now?"

His teenage self had been less courteous and far more eager around girls—well, *girl* singular, since Mellie was the only one to turn his world inside out. "I've learned a few things in the years we've been apart."

"I would hope so," Mellie said with a flirty smile, then she slipped through the door and out onto the porch. Her dark floral perfume lingered in the air, teasing him as much as her words and her smile.

His body stayed hyper-attuned to her as he sat a few feet away in his rental car. Every time she shifted, the tempting length of her legs flashed in his peripheral vision. The streetlights bounced off her hair, the curves of her face, the peach softness of her skin. More than once, he had to remind himself to focus on the road, not on the woman within touching distance.

"Where are we going first on our grand tour?" she

asked. "I was hoping maybe we could... I don't know... see that house that burned down. I mean, not to be morbid, but it's such a tragedy."

That hadn't been in his plan at all. A tour of the Kingstons' devastated property? No. Harris needed no reminders of that. "It's nothing to see, really."

"Well, I still think it would be interesting."

Odd that Mellie cared what a burned-out shell of a house looked like. But maybe she was like the rest of the town, concerned about the family, curious about what had happened. The Kingstons had only lived in Stone Gap for a few years, but they'd become a big part of the town already. Catherine was on the PTA, their kids played on the soccer and softball teams, and John volunteered at the community center from time to time. In the wake of the fire, the whole town seemed to have rallied around John and Catherine, which undoubtedly had made them feel like they really had a home in their adopted town.

There'd been a smattering of media attention to the fire, something Harris wanted to keep to a minimum. Any reporter worth his salt would eventually put the connection together, between Harris and the rebuild. And then there'd be questions about why the son of the man who had destroyed John's company was helping rebuild his house. Questions Harris didn't want to answer.

"I have someplace better in mind." He turned away from the main downtown area and took a side road that wound past antebellum houses and new construction, then down into a heavily wooded area that hung on for at least a mile before opening up to an expansive view of the ocean. On their right sat the Sea Shanty, a low-slung gray building with a wraparound deck that faced the ocean and served damned good seafood. The sound of pop music came from the open doors and windows.

"The Sea Shanty?"

"Best seafood you'll find in the area," he said. "Even better than Della's she-crab soup, but don't tell her I said that."

Mellie crossed her heart. "Never."

"I stopped in here on my first trip to Stone Gap, and I swear, I never found another meal like it anywhere else I went." He pulled into a parking space, then shut off the car. "You asked me about my favorite place in town, and this is it. Actually, it's the setting that's my favorite part. The food is just a bonus."

She sat back against the seat and took in the view of the restaurant. "That surprises me. I expected you to be…fancier."

"Because of my background."

"Well…yes. When we were dating, you always wanted to take me to some fancy restaurant with linen tablecloths and fifty forks."

"That's because I wanted to impress you."

Her face softened. "Harris, you impressed me the first minute I met you. I didn't need some overpriced steak to appreciate that."

Something in his chest tightened. Years ago, he'd felt like a bumbling fool around this wild, spontaneous, beautiful girl. A big part of that had been being a teenager, still growing into his height and his hormones, but part of it had been how self-assured Mellie always seemed. And even though he'd had the pedigreed background and the house with the Mercedes in the driveway, it was Mellie who seemed to have it all. "I impressed you? How?"

She waved off the question. "That's all ancient history, Harris. Let's go get dinner. I'm starving." Then she opened the car door and got out before he could come around the car.

She didn't want to talk about the past. Probably a damned good thing, because part of that past included Mellie cheating on him. He could still see her in the arms of another man, her head on his chest, his lips pressed against her hair. Harris needed to remember that when he got swept up in her smile or the scent of her perfume. Maybe she did, as she'd said, have a good explanation, and maybe he was just using all that teenage drama as an excuse to not get close to anyone again, especially the one woman who had always had his heart.

At the entrance to the Sea Shanty, she put a hand on his arm. And despite everything, his pulse jumped. "I want to be clear, Harris, that all I want is a good time tonight. We're just a couple of…friends reconnecting, sharing a few laughs. This is not a date. It's nothing permanent. It's one night, no more."

"Mellie, you don't strike me as a good-time-only woman. Especially considering you used to be married. That smacks of permanence." Once upon a time, he'd considered permanence with Mellie. But she'd chosen someone else.

"It's not permanent anything, not if you get divorced, too." She waited while he opened the restaurant door. The music came at them, louder and peppier, a jazzy cover of a pop song about meeting an old love. Ironic.

"Were you happy, though?" he asked. The bigger question was, *did he make you as happy as I thought you were with me?* The day after they broke up, Harris had driven to Boston, moved into his college dorm early and immersed himself in school. He'd thought he could forget Melanie in a new area, with enough books around him. He'd been wrong.

"Happiness is relative, don't you think?" Then she turned away, gave the hostess a nod and a second later, they were being seated at a table by the water.

"Gorgeous view, isn't it?" Harris said instead, staying in the safe area of small talk instead of dovetailing back into the personal. He wasn't sure if he meant the water, sparkling under the setting sun, or Mellie, with her hair touched with gold from the early-evening light and a pensive, peaceful look on her face as she watched the waves roll onto the beach.

"It's perfect. I've missed the water. I mean, I can see the Hudson and the Atlantic in New York, but it's a little grayer and not quite as pretty as it is here. Or as warm." She smiled, and that made him ten times happier that he'd chosen the seaside location.

"It's why it's my favorite place, too. I've always loved the water."

"I know." She dropped her attention to the menu.

"So, tell me. What is the secret to thinner thighs?"

He pretended to peruse his menu, bringing the mood back to light, airy. "Because I'm thinking it's not the lobster macaroni and cheese."

Mellie laughed. "Definitely not. The kale salad would be a great choice, though."

"I'd rather eat an oak tree than kale." He grimaced. "I'm not even sure that stuff can be classified as edible."

"Maybe if they cover it with cheese?" She grinned. "Almost anything is better with cheese."

"That is very, very true. But probably doesn't sell that many magazines."

She laughed again. "No. It definitely doesn't."

He laid his menu aside and straightened his fork and knife. "So, are you happy there? In New York, writing about kale salads and thin thighs?"

"It's not what I thought I'd be doing when I left college." She shrugged. "I got that degree in journalism, thinking I'd be the investigative reporter to find Jimmy Hoffa's body or something. Instead, I ended up at the magazine."

"So why not go find Jimmy Hoffa's body?"

She shook her head. "It's not that easy, Harris."

He thought of how long he had worked for his father, how many nights he had agonized over quitting. It hadn't been a fast decision or an easy one. But the minute he left his father's office after quitting—and being told he was no longer a part of the McCarthy family—Harris had felt a deep sense of relief. Little did he know how his mother would fall apart after he left. Some days, Harris thought maybe she'd died simply because she didn't want to live in that mausoleum of a house and marriage anymore. She'd once told her son she was proud he'd stood up to Phillip and had the courage to walk away. "Sometimes you just have to leap, Mellie. It's scary as hell, but it's better than being in a job you hate."

"I never said I hate my job."

"You never said you love it, either."

She shrugged. "How many people love their jobs? Anyway, I'm here for some lobster mac and cheese, not a discussion of my career choices."

He grinned. "That's a pretty rebellious choice, coming from the woman who wrote the book on thinner thighs."

She raised her water glass and mocked toasting him. "I'm not the rebel I once was, Harris."

"Neither one of us is the person we used to be, Mellie." He took a sip and glanced out over the water. He thought of the job he had done, the people it had impacted, the way he had been scrambling to change those lives ever since. "And I, for one, think that's a pretty damned good thing."

Chapter Six

Melanie couldn't remember the last time she had laughed this much. She'd forgotten about Harris's dry sense of humor. They'd talked around their past, discussing people they both knew, businesses in their old small town that had closed or expanded and the impact of the new highway that now cut through the center of town.

What they didn't talk about was their history. The feelings they'd had. The way things had ended. Melanie told herself it was better that way.

The truth came with complications. Pain. Heartache.

She could close her eyes and be right back in that moment, standing on the sidewalk, as devastated as she was relieved. The comfort of someone else's arms when all she'd really wanted was Harris's comfort.

Hearing his voice, speaking her name. Not Mellie that time, but the full *Melanie*, the word full of outrage and accusation. He hadn't paused long enough to hear her side. He'd assumed and decided she was guilty. And then, at the end, one hurt and shattered *Mellie* before he walked away.

And left her alone to process it all over the years that followed. She'd forgotten him, or maybe just convinced herself he wasn't who she thought he was.

But now, sitting across from her was the man she remembered. The same man she had fallen for in high school. Funny and charming and handsome as hell.

Which put her dangerously on the edge of losing her objectivity and focusing on kissing him again, not on the story that would save her career. Circle back, she told herself, to what mattered, and away from what didn't anymore.

"So how is Mrs. Josephs? Still threatening to run for senator?" Melanie said. The quirky older lady had lived two doors down from Abby and Melanie. A widow, she tended toward bright orange hats and even brighter dresses along with an ever-evolving collection of rain boots in whimsical patterns.

"She got remarried to that guy who owned the deli on the corner of Spruce," Harris said. "Took the whole town by surprise. They had a big wedding in the park, invited everyone in a three-county circle. She told everyone that was because she wanted everyone she knew to believe that happy endings exist."

Melanie laughed. "Who knew she was such a romantic? All I remember is her standing up at town meetings and ranting at the board of selectmen and calling them all—"

"A bunch of yellow-bellied toads who couldn't find their way out of a paper bag." Harris chuckled. "She was one colorful woman."

And a crazy romantic who believed in things like soul mates and world peace. Melanie didn't have time for such insanity. She was here for a story. Somehow she needed to redirect the conversation to the fire and what had happened. Real life, not some hopeless notions about happily-ever-after.

The waitress came by and asked them if they wanted anything else. Melanie looked down and realized they'd both cleaned their plates. Their conversation had been, as it had in the old days, so engrossing she'd barely tasted her dinner or the pinot grigio Harris had ordered. The man was too damned distracting.

"How about dessert to go?" Harris asked her. "We can take it down to the beach and eat it there."

A romantic stroll on the beach with a little sugar. Not distracting at all. If she was smart, she'd stay right here, in the well-lit, crowded restaurant and order bracing, non-romantic, non-beach-shareable coffee. "Sure. That sounds great."

Sounds like a mistake. And an easy way to forget why she was here.

"Two slices of the raspberry cheesecake, please," Harris said to the waitress. She nodded, then headed for the kitchen.

Damn. Raspberry cheesecake? She was definitely in trouble now. "You remembered my favorite dessert?"

"I remember a lot of your favorite things, Mellie."

And just like that, her mind was a decade in the past and she was in his arms, lying on a red plaid blanket spread beneath the stars. They'd made love that night, and when she came, he'd whispered in her ear that he remembered her favorite things to do. And he did. Very well.

Double damn. Now she'd gone down *that path* again in her head.

"Let me split the bill with you," she said, as she tugged a few bills out of her wallet. Nothing like going Dutch to spell not-a-romantic-date.

He waved off the money. "My date. My treat. When you plan our next date, you can pay, if you want."

A little zip of anticipation ran through her at the words *our next date*. Once again, she yanked her mind back to the present. Back to why she was here. Not to fall in love with Harris McCarthy again. Not to do anything other than redeem her career and get her life back on track.

After they left, they kicked their shoes off, leaving them beside the wooden boardwalk that led down to the soft sand and dark blue water. The sun had set, leaving the world in deepening shades of mauve and violet. The ocean lapped gently at the shore, in a quiet shush-shush song that soothed Melanie's stress. Harris seemed to relax by degrees the closer they got to the water, his steps slowing, his smile widening.

He always had loved the beach, as had she. Some of her favorite memories with Harris were on the water, with the sand under their toes and the Atlantic nudging at the rocky shore. Here they were, farther south on the same ocean, the shore sandier, warmer, more tropical, but still singing the same quiet song of the sea.

"If we go a little farther down," Harris said, "there's a grassy area that's perfect for a picnic."

"Sounds good." She fell into step beside him and tried to block the romantic part of the setting from her mind. The sooner she got this story, the sooner she could get her career back on track and be out of this too-perfect small town with this too-perfect man and back to her life in the city. Granted, it wasn't much of a life right now, but it was hers, and it was all she knew. "So, I hear they're starting a building project tomorrow for that family who lost everything in the fire."

"Yup."

That was it. One word. One short, sharp word. "Are you involved in that?"

"Yup."

He wasn't exactly opening up. That wasn't fitting well with her plan to get him to give her an exclusive interview. And his cologne smelled damned good, which was distracting. "Do you know the family well?"

"Here's that grassy area I was talking about." He strode up the beach a few feet and onto an oval of grass that diverted from the road and into the beach. Trees blocked the road, providing natural shade on sunny days and a dark canopy over the space now. Intimate. Cozy. "Have a seat."

Melanie dropped onto the grass, tucking her legs under her. Harris sat a couple feet away, his hand inches from hers, and that damned cologne luring her closer. "So...cheesecake," she said, too fast, too anxious, too nervous. To cover, she dived for the bag and wrestled with the small plastic container. She handed him a fork, then scooped up her own bite. "Oh my God. That is seriously good."

He grinned. "I knew you'd like it."

"You were right." She took another bite. The cheesecake was smooth, slightly tart, with the sweet kiss of raspberry sauce on the edges, and the crunch of a graham cracker crust. "I think I could eat this all day."

He ate a few bites of his slice, then leaned against the trunk of a tree. A fish jumped in the water, making a soft splash on the way down. "Makes me think of all those times we went to the shore when we were younger."

Years ago, they'd had picnics and Frisbee games and lazy afternoons under the sun. She had lain in his arms, planning for a future that had never happened. *Someday we're going to get married and leave this place*, Harris had said. *You're my everything, Mellie.*

She could close her eyes and hear his whisper in her ear, feel the warmth of his body against hers. She could imagine kissing him again, feeling him move against her and in her, their worlds coming together in one sweet moment—

And then came the reality of their breakup, and how he'd believed the worst about her without asking a single question. Harris McCarthy had abandoned her when she'd needed him most, and in the days since she ran into him, he hadn't spoken a word of apology. That alone should telegraph *don't fall for him again.*

"Yeah, those were great trips." She cut off another bite of cheesecake, paused a beat, then redirected the conversation. "So, what made you run into a burning building, anyway?"

Okay, so she wasn't going to win any awards for subtlety. That was fine with her. The sooner she got the story and got away from Harris—and these trips down memory lane—the better.

"People were in danger." He held up a bite of cheesecake. "Do you remember the cheesecake at Lou's? I think this one might be slightly better."

"Maybe. It's been a long time since I had the cheesecake at Lou's." She set her dessert aside and straightened to face him. "You had to have been very brave, Harris, to go in there."

He let out a gusty sigh. "I don't want to talk about it, Mellie. Not with you, not with anyone. Yeah, there was a fire, and yeah, I went in there and helped the family. But it's something anyone would have done for people in danger. The family's safe, we're starting work on reconstruction tomorrow, end of story."

Not exactly enough story to get her a Pulitzer. She thought about pressing him further, but she glanced at Harris's face and knew that look of determination that was in his eyes. He could be a stubborn man, and if he didn't want to talk, he wasn't going to. She needed a more circuitous route to what she wanted, while she tried to figure out why he was so prickly about the subject. "This is a beautiful place," she said. "I can see why you like it so much."

The change of subject relaxed Harris by a few degrees. "When I was a kid and I wanted to get away from my dad, I'd go down to that little creek by my house. I built forts, caught fish, did whatever I could to while away the hours and be in the quiet."

"I remember that creek." Narrow and winding, the creek near his house disappeared into a deeply wooded area that had led to the back of a small park. They'd spent many an afternoon exploring its banks. "Remember the day we caught the crayfish with our hands?"

He laughed. "You screamed and threw one at me."

"Hey, they had claws."

He arched a brow. "Their bodies are like three inches long. Not exactly life threatening."

"Maybe I just wanted you to think I was scared."

Harris shifted to face her, and the space between them seemed to disappear. "And why would you do that?"

Because when she was scared, he held her close. When she was upset, Harris kissed her on the temple and whispered words that eased everything, told her nothing could hurt her because he was there, and a part of her had needed that reassurance. Craved it. "I was scared of things with claws and antennae."

He brushed a tendril of hair away from her cheek. "Impossible. You're one of the smartest, bravest women I know."

Then how did I end up here, repeating history?

"I could say the same for you. I always thought you were…brilliant."

"You did?" He chuckled. "Not brilliant enough to avoid working for my father."

"Why did you?" Given how acrimonious their relationship had been, Melanie had expected Harris would do what he had told her he would do a hundred times when they'd talked about their future together—he would leave home the day he turned eighteen and never look back.

Harris shrugged. "Because as much as I wanted to get away from him, I also wanted him to love me. To approve of me."

His words held the ache of a deep sadness and long defeat. She wanted to reach for him, to soothe his hurts as he once had done hers. Instead she smoothed a hand over the grass, flattening, then watching the blades spring up again. "I get that. My mother is…hard to please."

"It's amazing to me that people who brought us into this world aren't happy with who we turned out to be. I thought going to work for him would make him proud." Harris's gaze went to the water, and his voice dropped into a softer range. "Instead, it turned me into someone I didn't want to be."

"What do you mean?" To her, he seemed the same as she remembered. Smart, funny, strong. Driven to do what was right, not necessarily what was popular. Except when it came to breaking her heart.

Harris picked up a fan-shaped clamshell, then arched back and flung it into the ocean. The shell disappeared in an incoming wave with a wink of white. "Working for my father required setting aside everything I believed about being a good person. I started waking up with my stomach in knots. I got headaches that wouldn't go away. It didn't take a genius to realize that was because I literally couldn't stomach my job."

"Why?"

"Because working for my father required me to destroy other people. Businesses brought him in to do analyses and consulting. If my father said fire these ten people, they fired them. If he said close this branch, they closed that branch. It made them profitable, but..." He shook his head. "There was always a cost to pay, not in dollars, but in people's lives."

She thought of the story she wanted to do. The price she was willing to pay to get her career back on track. No. She refused to feel guilty. The publicity could help the Kingston family with donations, and Harris would be long gone by the time the piece was published. And maybe Harris wouldn't mind it so much if the article painted him as the hero he clearly was.

Harris cleared his throat. "Anyway, once I started building houses, I felt like I had a job that made a difference. The end."

A part of her suspected that hadn't been the end. She could hear the evasive notes in Harris's voice. Something about his story didn't ring quite true, but what that was, she couldn't tell. The days when she knew him as well as she knew herself had ended a long time ago.

"At least you had a dad. My dad died when I was

born." Melanie said. "I remember being so jealous of the other kids with their dads that one time, I made up a dad who was in the military, just so that the other girls would think he was a hero or something.

"I guess it's no wonder I went into the career I did, since I've been spinning the truth since I was a kid." She hesitated for a moment. "I loved my sister, but Abby was always the perfect one, and nothing I did ever seemed to measure up. Even at home I'd try to make myself seem smarter, better, nicer. I'd say anything to impress my mom, to get her to notice me, even if my words were a stretch."

"And sometimes lies are for good reason," he said. "To protect others."

"Others like who?"

Instead of answering, he leaned over and opened his arms, welcoming her to lean against his chest. Melanie didn't want to, didn't want to get close or fall for him again. Because being this close and this alone with Harris definitely awakened feelings she'd thought were long dead. Feelings that would only complicate everything. But the moment had bonded them in a way, the two of them misunderstood and lost years ago and now brought back together by some strange coincidence of being in the same place at the same time. She wanted a little of that past, and a little of him, and a little of what she had loved in the years they had dated. Just for now.

She leaned into the solid wall of his chest. He was warm, and his cologne—a different one from when they were younger—had sharp notes of spice that drew her even closer.

"Let's watch the day come to a close, Mellie, and not talk about the past." He pressed a tender kiss to the top of her head, and she was lost. Lost in his arms, lost in the moment, lost in the soft song of the ocean. Lost in him, all over again.

Tomorrow, she told herself, tomorrow was soon enough to get back to work.

Chapter Seven

Harris had expected maybe a handful of people to show up to help tear down the rest of the Kingston house and start erecting the new one. But when he arrived bright and early Thursday morning, he found three dozen volunteers being sorted into different jobs by Jack Barlow. All of the Barlow brothers were here, along with Mac's wife, Savannah, who owned a business renovating houses.

Della and Bobby Barlow were handing out donuts and coffee to everyone who had shown up. The Kingston family stood to the side, with gratitude filling their faces. Catherine had a hand on the shoulders of two of her kids, and her littlest one—John Jr., was pressed up against his mother's legs. Tears glimmered in Catherine's eyes, and even John had a hard time keeping it together.

The devastation became clearer, more heartbreaking, in the light of day. What had once been the front half of a rambling ranch house had crumbled into a few ghostly pillars and piles of gray ash, mounded over the remains of the Kingstons' lives. A lamp here, a pan there and then a blackened shell where the bedrooms had been. In those spaces, a few things could be salvaged, but almost everything would need to be replaced. The fund at the Stone Gap bank was growing every day, but Harris made a mental note to call in a few favors from some of his fat-wallet clients and see if he couldn't boost that number even more.

Harris stopped beside Jack. The former military officer had kept his trim frame and short hair. He wore a perpetual smile and glanced at his pregnant wife from time to time, clearly overjoyed at the prospect of fatherhood. A trickle of envy ran through Harris. For some strange reason, he wished he had a reason to stay in town and see the next generation of Barlows grow up. Insane.

"I had no idea this many people would show up," Harris said.

Jack grinned. "That's the kind of town Stone Gap is. Ernie's Hardware is donating a bunch of supplies so we can get started right away. My mom said you were talking about holding a fund-raiser to drum up the rest of the money we need to finish the project. She said she's on board for whatever you want to do."

"That's fabulous. Truly."

Jack looked at the gray, crumbling wreckage that had once been a three-bedroom house. "Such a shame.

When folks heard the Kingstons didn't have insurance, they wanted to help as much as they could."

That was small-town community at its finest, and something Harris had seen so rarely in his life, he'd given up on believing a world like that existed. Those years working for his father had left a jaded edge on most of Harris's thoughts.

Harris clapped Jack on the shoulder. Like his brothers, he was a good guy, a cornerstone in this town. "I know the family appreciates it all."

Jack shrugged. "Least we can do. One of these days, it could be you or me."

"Amen. Thanks again." Harris saw a white van pulling into the driveway, a television station logo emblazoned on the side. Great. Media. The last thing anyone needed. Harris cursed. "I'll get rid of them."

Jack put a hand on his arm. "Before you run off the TV crew, I know the Kingstons want to keep this private, but honestly, if we're going to raise the funds we need to, a little publicity can't hurt."

A *little* publicity Harris could live with, and something he'd talked to John and Catherine about when he set up the trust fund at the bank. Inevitably, reporters would ask. Overwhelmed by what they had been through, the Kingstons had asked him to handle the media.

Harris was good with a mention in the local paper about donations. But a prying reporter who asked too many questions, he didn't want. The only way to be sure it was the former and not the latter was to handle the interview himself. The last thing he wanted was for anyone to make the link between Phillip McCarthy and the shuttering of John Kingston's business.

Harris approached the news van just as a slim brunette woman climbed out of the passenger's seat. Another man slid open the side door and settled a camera on his shoulder. The big, dark eye swiveled around the scene before them—the crew readying themselves with gloves and hard hats to begin the demolition, the order of lumber being stacked on one side of the yard and the eager people listening to Jack's directions.

The brunette turned to the cameraman. "Ready, Ed? Let's start with the family. See if we can—"

"Excuse me. Are you here to do a story on the Kingston family?" Harris asked.

"Yes, yes we are. Do you know them?" The brunette looked past him, her gaze still scanning the crowd. The breeze lifted the collar of her shirt but didn't move her hair-sprayed hair a single millimeter. "Could you point out Mr. or Mrs. Kingston?"

"I'm the family spokesperson," Harris said. "They are, understandably, traumatized by what happened and would prefer not to talk about it with the media just yet."

The brunette's attention swiveled toward him, a laser beam of bright eyes and a new smile. "And you are?"

"A concerned friend."

"I'm Barbara Gold, from TV 13." She glanced over her shoulder at Ed, who handed her a microphone, then nodded. Ed shuffled closer, and before Harris could protest, Barbara thrust the microphone under her chin.

"You're a friend of the Kingston family, who lost everything they owned in a terrible fire last Tuesday. Can you tell us about what happened that night?"

"There was a fire. I don't have any more details than that, I'm sorry." He was lying, but this brunette with her lacquered hair didn't need to know the truth. Nor did he intend to give her any kind of interview, Jack's advice be damned. "I need to get back to the demolition project."

Barbara put a hand on his arm, then withdrew it just as quickly. "I heard there was a stranger who ran into the house and rescued the family from certain death. Do you know who that was?"

"No, I don't." The eye of the camera seemed to loom over him, threatening to expose him as a liar. *You're the whole reason they were penniless. The reason John was drunk and depressed. You didn't save them. You practically handed John a match.* "I really have to help with the demolition project. I know the family would appreciate it if you would respect their privacy right now and give them some time before they do an interview."

He was holding out a carrot he never intended to give the reporter. But if it was enough to get her to climb back in that van and leave, then he'd say almost anything.

The reporter considered his words for a long moment, her gaze flicking between Harris and the people starting work on the charred remains of the house. Finally, she looked over her shoulder at her cameraman.

"Just grab some B-roll and then we can head over to that five-car pileup on I-95."

Harris held his sigh of relief until the TV crew left a few minutes later. He wouldn't be able to hold the media off forever. But with any luck, some other story would grab their attention. By the time they did a follow-up, Harris would be back in Connecticut and the Kingstons would be happily ensconced in their new home.

Harris turned back toward the job site, then stopped. In the midst of the crew, he saw a familiar figure. She was smiling and talking to Della, and something in Harris's chest clenched.

Mellie.

She peeled off from Della a moment later, heading for a stack of shovels leaning against Jack's truck. A pale blue V-neck T-shirt drew his attention away from her face, then down the curves outlined by dark-wash jeans. He crossed to her, grabbing a shovel of his own as he went. "What are you doing here?"

"Helping." She held up the shovel in her gloved hands and gave him a grin. She looked too beautiful to be shoveling chunks of burned wood, with a bare minimum of makeup and her dark hair back in a ponytail, which made her look younger, sweeter.

Harder to resist.

"Well, that's good," he said, though he knew she would be a distraction he didn't need. He'd already vowed after last night's walk on the beach that he wasn't going to get too close to her. He'd held her to his chest, kissed her forehead, and just like that, he'd been eighteen and head over heels again.

When he'd leaned in to kiss her, she'd jerked away, claiming she needed to sleep, and had asked him to drive her back to the inn. They'd exchanged a handful of small talk on the ride, then peeled off in separate directions once they were inside the bed-and-breakfast. He'd tossed and turned all night, painfully aware she lay in a bed just down the hall. And that she had brushed him off.

Mellie had made it clear the date was platonic. The rational side of him remembered they lived in two different states, and his time in Stone Gap was limited. That didn't stop the irrational side from wishing he'd done a lot more than hold her on the beach.

"I'm not really handy," Mellie said, drawing his attention back to the present. "But I can shovel or tear down stuff. Get some stress worked out." She hoisted the shovel and flexed her arm. "I ate my spinach this morning and everything."

He laughed. Okay, so maybe having her around would be nice. Really nice. "We could use all the help we can get."

They walked toward the remains of the house. Several people greeted Harris as he passed, and he nodded a friendly hello in return. "Does everyone in this town know you?"

"When I built that house down the road, I spent a lot of time in town. People got used to seeing me around."

"So you've grown up into a dependable adult?"

The words had the lilt of a joke, but he heard something else shading the undertones. He shot Mellie a glance, but sunglasses hid her eyes. "I'd like to think so."

"I did, too." The last she said in a whisper, then she stopped walking and let out a gasp. "God, this is horrible."

He stood beside her, taking in the scene as she did. A crumbling, blackened skeleton of a home lay in the center of a ring of oak and maple trees. The front door had oddly survived, even as the jamb around it had been lost to the fire. The red entryway lay on the ground, facedown, defeated and sad among the rest of the gray. Odd shapes buried under ash and fallen timbers revealed the life that had once been here—a coffee table, a sofa, a kitchen table, a set of three twin beds, two at an L-angle together in the first bedroom, the other sunken into the ground beside a dresser that seemed to be covered with one large black handprint.

Mellie shook her head. "It's a wonder anyone survived. They owe that to you, Harris."

"It was a bad fire, but it started in the living room, which gave us enough time to get everyone out of the house. Anyone would have done the same." He could still smell the smoke, feel the heat of the flames. Standing here, beside the very door he had flung open just a few days ago, his heart began to pound, his throat constricting. One minute later, and there'd be more than just the remains of furniture in this space. For the thousandth time, he thanked God he'd been in the right place at the right time.

And in the next breath, he remembered no one would

have been in this situation if not for him. He could run into a hundred fires and it wouldn't be enough.

Catherine Kingston climbed over the fallen timbers and crossed to Harris. She drew him into a tight hug, then pulled back. She was a small woman, short and painfully thin, but when she smiled, she lit up a room. She had a fierce love for her children and husband, and from what he knew of her, she had weathered some massive storms in her life. Her face was lined with worry and stress, her eyes shadowed by nights without sleep, but her smile held gratitude and relief. "Harris. I can't thank you enough for organizing this and for...earlier." She nodded toward the departing television van.

"I didn't do much, Catherine. Put a bug in Jack Barlow's ear, and he and his family ran with it."

Catherine waved his words off, then turned to Mellie. "Don't let this man pretend he isn't some kind of amazing, incredible person. Not only did he save all of us from that fire, dragging us out of our beds in the middle of the night, but he set this whole thing up and is running a fund-raiser and everything. He's got the housing plans nearly approved by the town council and has already started delivering the supplies. We didn't have insurance, and I have no idea where we'd be without Harris."

"You give me too much credit, Catherine," he said. He didn't deserve the way she looked at him, as if he was part superhero and part Norse god. He didn't deserve the kudos for something that was really a townwide effort. And he sure as hell didn't deserve to be thanked when he was the one who'd bankrupted John Kingston.

"I've known Harris a long time," Mellie said. "I'm not surprised to hear he did all that. Most of the time, he's the kind of guy you rely on in a crisis."

Most of the time. That curious tone underlaid her words again.

"I'd say all the time," Catherine said. "He's one hell of a great guy. John can't stop telling everyone what a blessing Harris has been to our family."

They were talking about him like he wasn't even here. He thought of walking away, but he knew Catherine, and knew she'd gush about him to Mellie for a solid half hour. The majority of it would surely be misconceptions that Melanie didn't need to hear. "Catherine, why don't we start seeing what we can salvage?"

"It's all so…overwhelming." She sighed and ran a hand through her hair. "The kids…they lost so much. I'm afraid there's nothing worth saving."

"There's always something worth saving," Mellie said softly. "Let me help, too."

That hadn't been his plan. He'd figured Mellie would go help the others doing demolition, not tag along and make him think about her altogether too much. Or wonder what message lay beneath what she'd said this morning. The way she'd pulled away last night, the chill that existed between them.

"Thank you," Catherine said. She laid a hand on Mellie's arm. "I hope Harris knows how lucky he is to have you."

"Oh, we're not—I mean—" Mellie blushed. "We're just friends."

Just friends. Ouch. The reality slap hit him hard. And reminded him that maybe that was for the best.

He'd seen her with someone else, getting touched, kissed. Just when he'd been about to tell her he wanted to spend the rest of his life with her. Granted, they'd been kids, young and immature, but the moment never quite left the recesses of his mind. He'd be a fool to fall for her again.

So he focused on the burned house and the people who needed his help.

Ahead of him, Catherine climbed over the thick beam that had once been the spine of the house, dodged a crumbling armchair. Harris and Mellie followed. He tried to ignore the stench of burned plastic.

Catherine stopped in the first bedroom, standing among the skeletal two-by-fours that had framed the closet. "I hope it's still here," she whispered. "If I can find that, maybe the kids will…"

"What?" Harris asked.

"Please let it be here." She bent down and began to move the burned clothing, charred toys, crumbling boxes. Harris started to help, pushing things aside even as they crumbled in his hands. Ash flew into the air around them like a gray snowstorm.

Catherine dug, her movements more frantic as each second passed, then she turned over a metal bin and let out a gasp. "Oh, thank goodness." She turned and rose, and in her arms was a stuffed black bear, well worn and loved, with a missing patch on his forehead and frayed edges on his paws. Catherine's eyes welled. "It's her bear."

In that moment, the love Catherine had for her children was as real and tangible as the stuffed bear. He'd never known a love like that, at least not from his own parents. His father too exacting and cruel, and his mother too afraid to rock the boat. She had died afraid and alone, and that was another moment Harris had yet to forgive himself for.

"Let's get it cleaned off," Harris said. He brushed the bear's fur, and it gradually changed from ash gray to black. "At the end of the day, I can take it to get cleaned. I'm sure the dry cleaner can do something to make it like new again."

"Thank you, Harris," Catherine said, clutching the bear to her chest, heedless of the tears sliding down her cheeks. "Thank you."

He glanced at Mellie and saw her eyes were misty, too. The three of them stood there in the wreckage for a moment, two of them moved to tears over the discovery of a treasure, and one feeling as if he was somewhere he didn't belong.

Melanie watched Catherine hand the stuffed bear to her daughter, a girl around Jake's age. The joy on the little blonde's face lit the dark space like sunshine. It was a beautiful moment, the kind that could be a Hallmark card, although there was no occasion to hand over a greeting that said, *here's what we rescued from the fire. Sorry you lost everything else.*

This could have been her sister's house. Her sister's children losing everything. It could have been Abby digging through the rubble, searching for answers, hope, new beginnings.

Or worse, it could have been her own family. For just a second, Melanie stood there, closed her eyes and imagined a little girl with Harris's smile and her eyes. A little girl who was never going to exist. She knew that, she'd accepted it, but still there were days—

Days when she wished for a different ending than the one she'd been dealt at eighteen. It had been the happiest moment of her life, quickly ruined by the most devastating moment of her life. And Harris hadn't been there, hadn't listened.

Catherine Kingston waved to Harris and brought him over with her and the children. He bent down and started talking to two of them, a boy of about seven and a girl about five. And something in Melanie's heart began to ache.

Would he have been a good father? One that loved his children, hugged them when they skinned a knee, held them tight when they were scared and let them go when they wanted to spread their wings?

No. She couldn't let her mind go back there. Losing that baby had been a blessing in disguise. She'd been so overjoyed when she found out she was pregnant, even though she was young. But then she'd lost the baby, and told herself that she'd been too young to be a single mother anyway. Plus Harris had disappeared from her life, never knowing the truth. He'd believed the lie instead of giving her a chance. That wasn't the kind of man who should be the father of her child.

Melanie should be taking some notes, asking Catherine some questions, pursuing the story instead of dwelling on what-ifs that never got to be. Instead, she watched the family moment a little while longer, then turned back to start shoveling the debris into a wheelbarrow. Her eyes burned from the ashes she kicked up and the lingering acrid scent of smoke.

Della Barlow came by and handed Melanie an icy water bottle. Dozens of volunteers swarmed around the site like bees in a field of daisies. A low hum of conversation, peppered with the occasional joke, kept the mood productive but light. "It's wonderful that you're helping, and on your vacation, no less."

"I just felt so bad about what happened." And with that, she felt bad about lying. Again. What would it be like to just be honest with everyone? Abby? Her mother? Della?

Harris?

Okay, that was insanity talking. Maybe the fumes were getting to her brain. She set the water down and scooped up some more charred wood.

Della surveyed the house and shook her head. "It is terrible. But the family is safe and together, and that's what matters. Things can be replaced—people can't."

"They look like a wonderful family." Across the way, Melanie spied a pale, thin man talking to Harris while they pulled debris out from the ruins. He kept glancing at his family as he worked. "Is that Mr. Kingston?"

"Yes. John's a great guy. Started a barbershop in town. He used to own some kind of company, and it got shut down, so he started all over again, as a barber. I think he used to work for his dad's barbershop when he was a kid. But starting over is never easy, and I know he's been heartbroken over losing his company and having to lay all those people off." Della sighed. "That family has been struggling for so long. And to have this on top of everything else… I'm just glad the town is helping out."

Melanie made a mental note to find out more about John Kingston, how he knew Harris and, most of all, why Harris had been there that night. The Kingstons seemed like a nice, normal family. Had it been faulty wiring? A spark from the fireplace? What happened that night?

The Kingstons didn't know her at all, and the chances of them opening up to a stranger were slim. Her best route for the information was Harris. Except Harris kept throwing up roadblocks. He'd never been a secretive guy, at least not when she'd known him. Why did this particular event have him clamming up? Was he that uncomfortable with the *bona-fide hero* part of it?

To get him to trust her, to open up, meant spending more time alone with him. Which meant trying not to be tempted by him. Even now, watching him across the way, she noticed the muscles rippling under his T-shirt, the way his jeans hugged his long, lean legs. The way his smile caused her belly to flip and tempted her to get closer.

Jack blew a whistle, announcing lunch for everyone. Melanie jerked her attention away from Harris, then leaned her shovel against a post and walked with Della over to a set of makeshift picnic tables. A rainbow of folding chairs lined the sides.

Dylan and Abby emerged from Dylan's truck, with Cody and Jake bringing up the rear. Jake barreled toward his aunt, a little dynamo speeding across the grassy yard. "Aunt Melanie! We came to help!"

"That's awesome. We can always use extra help, especially from strong boys like you." Melanie ruffled his hair. He beamed up at her, all smiles and love, the sweetest little boy she'd ever met.

"The boys had a half day at school," Abby said, "and Mavis is handling the community center, so we thought we'd bring some extra hands to help." She looked past her sister and smiled. "Harris, how nice to see you."

"Hi, Abby and crew." Harris slipped into place beside Melanie as if he belonged there. He shook hands with Dylan and traded small talk with the boys, asking about the community center, the new basketball court Harris had donated, overseeing the installation himself. As he had with Catherine, Harris brushed off the praise and gratitude from Dylan and Cody. "We're all sitting down for some lunch, courtesy of the amazing culinary skills of Della Barlow, if you guys want to join us."

"Can I sit next to you, Aunt Melanie?" Jake asked. "Please?"

"Of course you can." She gave him a grin. "You're my favorite lunch companion in the whole wide world."

"Harris, I've been practicing my kicking!" Jacob

swung his leg back and forth. "Just like you showed me. See?"

"That's awesome, buddy." Harris bent down to Jake's level and met the little boy's gaze with a serious, adult face. "You want to keep your place foot, that's the one that doesn't kick, right square with the ball. That helps you aim your kick and score a goal."

Harris had donated a basketball court? Was teaching her nephew how to play soccer? Who was this man? He'd become some kind of superhero in the years they'd been apart.

Where was that man when I needed him? The deep ache in her chest, the one she had pushed to the side a thousand times since that day she'd left the clinic, roared to life, choked her throat.

"Let's find a seat, Jake," Melanie said, taking her nephew's hand and tugging him away from Harris, the new town father/benefactor/saint. As they settled down at the picnic table, Jake climbed into the chair on Melanie's left, Abby and Dylan sat on the opposite side, and Cody wandered off to sit with some kids he knew. That left Harris, dropping into the seat on her right.

Close enough that she could still catch the scent of his cologne. See the small patch of stubble he had missed when he shaved this morning. Watch the way his fingers flexed as he poured a glass of lemonade, then handed the pitcher down the table.

"Melanie? Did you hear me?"

Melanie drew herself up and focused on her sister. She tucked her sunglasses on top of her head. "Sorry, Abs. I was daydreaming."

Abby laughed. "No problem. I was just asking if you had time to go with me to a dress fitting tomorrow morning. We can do the final fitting on my dress and see if yours needs anything."

"Sure, that would be great." She'd ordered her maid of honor dress online and had it shipped to Abby's house.

"I can't believe I'm about to get married." Abby grinned at Dylan and took his hand. He leaned over and kissed her, with more love in that sweet, short gesture than Melanie had ever seen between two people. Abby held his gaze for a moment, then turned back. "Harris, if you're still in town, you should come to our wedding. It's nothing fancy, more of a picnic in the town park kind of thing. We'd love to have you there, especially after all you have done for the town and our boys."

Harris glanced at Melanie. For a second, she wanted to tell him *no, don't come*. Because being at a wedding meant him asking her to dance, which meant being in his arms, and she already knew that Harris was a very, very good dancer. "I'd love to be there," he said. "If the maid of honor can promise me one dance."

Damn. He'd read her mind. She really needed to start wearing sunglasses more often. Go all mysterious and silent. She slid them back over her eyes.

Jake saved her from having to answer by tugging on her sleeve. "Aunt Melanie, are you coming to my soccer game? It's on Saturday. I'm gonna get a goal."

"Of course I'll go, Jake. I wouldn't miss it for the world."

She turned her attention to Jake for the rest of the

lunch, but her awareness remained on the man sitting so close to her, she could feel the heat from his body. Harris chatted with Abby and Dylan about the rebuild of the Kingston home, drawing her into the conversation from time to time.

As soon as Melanie had finished her sandwich, she got to her feet. "I've got an interview to go do," she said to her sister. "I'll see you for dinner tonight?"

Abby nodded. "Sounds great. I'm making spaghetti."

That elicited a cheer from Jake. Melanie gave her nephew a kiss on the forehead. "Maybe after dinner, we can practice soccer in the backyard, Jake."

"Yay! I can practice my kicking more. Did you see me kick? I kicked really hard!" Jake's enthusiasm bubbled out of him like a volcano. "Can we play with my puppy, too? He's so funny when I throw the ball."

"Sure, whatever you want, kiddo." Melanie stood there a moment, in awkward silence. "Uh, Harris, I guess I'll see you later."

Her face flushed, and her words stumbled. She'd been unsettled around him ever since she'd seen him with the Kingston kids and Jake. The sentimental side of her kept imagining a future they'd never had.

Because she'd lost the baby. And Harris had seen her being comforted and assumed the worst about her. She already had a mother who did that. She didn't need to get involved with a man who did, too.

"I'm looking forward to it," Harris said. A genuine, warm smile spread across his features. His gaze met hers and held.

Even long after Melanie had gotten in her car and driven across town to interview Stone Gap's oldest living resident, that smile lingered on the fringes of her memory. Everything about him did. Damn that man. Once again, Harris McCarthy was screwing up her plans for her life.

Chapter Eight

Harris grabbed a bottle of beer out of the fridge, then headed down the hall of the inn. The long day clearing away the wreckage had drawn to a close when the sun set and working on the site became too dangerous. Harris had gone back to his room and set to work ordering plywood, insulation and windows and scheduling a concrete pour. His attention wandered a thousand times.

Probably because he'd been listening for Mellie's steps in the hallway. She must have stayed late after dinner at her sister's house, because the clock ticked past ten and she still hadn't come back to the inn. Finally, he'd given up on his work and gone downstairs to enjoy the evening air. Or at least, that's what he told himself.

Mavis was asleep in the back bedroom of the inn, and the other guests had checked out earlier today, leaving the building mostly empty. So when the front door finally opened a little after ten thirty, Harris's heart skipped a beat.

Why did he torture himself like this? They had ended things long ago, and each of them had a life in a different state, a different world. And yet sometimes, the part of him that remembered an impatient, more immature self at eighteen thought perhaps the past could be rewritten. Lord knew he'd made enough mistakes in his younger years—and a few as an adult—that he would do over if he could. He'd been given a chance to fix things with Mellie—could he really let that opportunity go?

He turned and saw Mellie in the doorway. Her gaze caught his, and for a second, he worried she would go straight to bed and not talk to him. She leaned toward the stairs, as if she'd decided to avoid him.

"Want a beer?" he said, too fast. "And then you can tell me the secrets to long life. You interviewed the town's oldest living resident, right? I'd love to hear about it."

Too much? Too desperate? Too insane? Damn. What was it with this woman, that all his thoughts became a jumbled mess whenever she was around? He forgot about the past, forgot about their broken history, and couldn't think about anything other than being with her.

Mellie came down the hall, depositing her purse and notepad on the hall table. She looked tired, as if the long day had had more challenges than just an interview and a family dinner. "I'd love a beer."

He headed into the kitchen, grabbed a second one, opened it and handed it to her. She took a long drink, then gestured toward the back porch. They went outside and sank into the twin Adirondack chairs.

"Cheers," she said and clinked her bottle with his. The faint chitter of crickets came from the shrubs. Mellie sipped her beer, and the tension in her shoulders relaxed by degrees. "So, did you guys get a lot of work done on the house?"

"More than I expected. All the demo is done, and tomorrow we get to start building." He'd pushed the town commissioners to do a rush approval on the plans. A generous donation to help build a new ballfield in town had helped move that along. Harris knew he'd have to make up all these expenses down the road, but he lived pretty inexpensively in a humble apartment, and kept his business costs low just so he could do things like this.

In the end, the money meant a family would have a home in a few weeks, instead of cramming into a motel room or a relative's basement for months. It had been a chaotic day, but the Barlow brothers had kept the project under control.

Dozens of Stone Gap residents had been there yesterday from sunup to sundown, working until it got too dark. John and his family had only been residents for a few years, and yet the town embraced them like long-lost cousins. For a second, Harris wondered what it would be like to make this town his permanent home. The idea appealed quite a bit.

Could he set up a home base here? And still complete the mission he'd had in his heart ever since he quit working for his father? Could he finally, after John's house was complete, give himself a moment to live his own life, and still make reparations to the lives he had ruined? Deep questions for a dark night, and questions he couldn't answer.

"I talked with Della about having a fund-raiser on Saturday to make enough money for all the rest of the things the family is going to need—clothes, furniture, dishes," Harris said. "We're thinking of having a barbecue here at the inn."

"That sounds like fun." Mellie rested her feet on the edge of her chair and sank down a little. "I can see if Saul wants me to write up something about it for the paper. I'll talk to him tomorrow when I turn in my story."

"Do you still write everything in longhand first?" Back in high school, Mellie had kept yellow legal pads everywhere—in her backpack, on her nightstand, in the kitchen, pretty much wherever she went. He was always finding them scattered in her wake, her handwriting, neat and tight, flowing across the page with words and ideas and imagination.

She turned and smiled at him. "I do. I know it's probably a huge waste of time, but my brain just connects with the words better that way. At least on the stories that matter."

"And which ones are those?"

"Not the ones about kale salad and thin thighs. Those I always wrote on the computer. I still have a

stack of legal pads that are blank and waiting for something with substance." She picked at the label of the
beer bottle, peeling it away in one long strip. "I went
to work at that magazine, hoping I could write some
things with depth. I did one piece on college graduates
that had some meat to it. I hoped they'd let me write
more like it, but then they hired a new editorial director, and we went to more fluff and less substance."

The Mellie he remembered wouldn't have been
much about fluff. She may have been bold and adventurous—and he had loved that part of her when he still
lived under his father's thumb—but she hadn't been
the kind that cared about having her clothes make a
statement. She'd never worried about wearing the most
fashionable jeans or having the right color eye shadow.
"Well, either way, your sister is proud as hell of you.
Every time I talk to her, it's all she talks about."

Mellie scoffed. "If she only knew." The words were
a whisper under her breath. Harris wasn't even sure
Mellie meant to speak them aloud.

"What do you mean?"

She shook her head. Picked at the beer label.
Avoided his gaze.

"Mellie…" He waited until she lifted her gaze to
his. "Talk to me."

A long moment passed. The weight that had lifted
from her shoulders returned. She took a long sip of the
beer, then let out a sigh. "I lost my job at the magazine
and never told my family."

"You did? When?"

"A year ago. Around the same time as my divorce."

She laid a strip of label on the arm of the chair, then started in on the next section. "I started arguing that the magazine needed to run stories with more substance. In response, the new editorial director said I didn't fit the direction of the magazine anymore, and she let me go."

Mellie had a lovely writing style, with a light touch that brought life to her essays, papers or short stories. How could anyone fail to see the value of her and her skills? "Did you move on to another magazine? One that would appreciate your talent?"

She scoffed. "Writing about diets and moisturizers isn't exactly a prestigious résumé. And in a city like New York, there are millions of writers. I took on some freelancing work and lived off my savings, and, well, now I'm here, working for the *Stone Gap Gazette*, at least for a little while. Maybe doing that can build up my résumé a bit in other areas—and help my bank balance at the same time."

Mellie had to be in bad financial shape if she was taking on a job while she was on vacation. Harris wondered if he had any contacts he could call, maybe help her find a new job. Except he was in the construction industry, which was about as far from writing as a person could get. He hated not being able to help her, though.

She took another sip, then set the bottle beside the curled paper. "Either way, I don't think profiling the town's oldest resident is going to get me into a prestigious paper or magazine, but it's a start."

"And it's better than writing about miracle weight-loss techniques, right?" He grinned, but she didn't return his smile.

"Yeah." Mellie let out a sigh, then got to her feet and leaned against the railing. She turned away from him and faced the dark expanse of lawn and lake, a landscape that seemed to disappear into nothing. "I'm glad you left your dad's practice and went after your dreams, Harris. I wonder sometimes if I'm still trying to find mine."

The soft, vulnerable admission drew him to her side. He didn't touch her, just filled the space on her right. "Maybe you just got a little off track, Mellie. You're an amazing writer, and I think you still have some great stories to tell."

She shrugged.

His arms ached to hold her, to draw her into his chest like he used to do, and to inhale the sweet fragrance of her perfume. To ease the stress in her eyes and make everything better. "You know, I read those pieces about the first year in New York for those women college graduates."

She turned to him, her face lit with surprise. "You did? Why didn't you tell me?"

"Well, because it kind of seems like stalking to google your ex-girlfriend." A whip-poor-will called out in the night air, the familiar song sounding lonely and distant. Harris knew that feeling. All these years he had been estranged from his family, on a one-man quest to set things right again with the people his father had hurt. The only woman he'd ever truly felt at home with was standing right in front of him, but she might as well have been a million miles away. "When I first saw you again, I was curious. So I looked up what you'd been writing, and I came across that series of articles. It was beautiful, Mellie. Heartfelt and honest and heartbreaking, all at the same time."

"Yeah, well, it's not the kind of thing editors want from me."

He touched her jaw, met her gaze. "*One* editor. Not all editors. You're a wonderful writer, Mellie, when you trust yourself."

"Trust myself?" Her brows furrowed. "I do that."

He paused a moment, then said what he'd been meaning to say ever since he found out about her career at a light and frothy magazine. He'd been surprised to find out the untamable Mellie ended up at a magazine as shallow as a wading pool. "I think it's safe to write about kale salad, and the woman I remembered never played it safe."

The Mellie he remembered took chances. She was the first to leap into a swimming hole, the one person he knew who wasn't afraid of the dark or bears in the woods or anything else. Sure, she'd broken a few rules along the way—okay, almost all of them—by skipping school or swiping a pack of gum from the corner store, but there'd always been this sense of adventure, of danger about her.

She'd been the one he wanted to be. The one who ran with things, and didn't fall into the prescribed life someone else had laid out for her. Maybe he'd been channeling a little of that the day he quit working for his father. "Where did that side of you go? It's like one day you woke up and changed into someone else. What happened to the risk-taking girl I fell in love with?"

She shook her head and turned away from him. "You don't know me anymore, Harris. You don't know my life. Risks can get you hurt, and I've had enough of that, thank you very much."

Something had happened to her, something that kept inserting itself between them. Whatever it was had tamed the wild in Mellie, but it also extinguished a lot of the light that he loved about her. "Once upon a time, you could tell me anything."

"And once upon a time, you broke my heart."

He scoffed. "Me? You were the one I caught with someone else."

"And what did you do? Believed the worst about me instead of talking to me. So don't stand here, Harris, and act like you're someone I can trust. You broke up with me, not the opposite."

"Then tell me now—what you were doing that night?"

"It doesn't matter anymore, Harris. It's in the past. And I'm over it." But tears shimmered in her eyes and her words shook. Ten years may have gone by, but the night still stung. "It's too late to rewrite history."

"I don't want to rewrite the past." They'd been young, immature, and maybe it was best to leave all that in the rearview mirror. He wished he could go back and handle it better, not let his pride and temper keep him from listening. "But maybe we could start over, in the here and now."

"You know how you could help me out? Change my

life? Make it up to me?" She closed the space between them and raised her chin. "Tell me what happened the night of the fire. Tell me why you're doing so much for a family you barely know."

It took him a second to make the connection, to realize she wasn't asking for a second chance for them. She was asking him to give her a second chance at her career. "Is that all I am to you? A scoop for some big-city paper?"

"What, do you feel like I'm using you? Well, why shouldn't I? All I ever was to you was a way to piss off your father. I was the wild girl he disapproved of, the one person he would have done anything to get rid of. Instead, you did that yourself. The one night I needed you most, you left me." She gathered up the scraps of label, crushing them into a ball in her fist. "So let's not pretend that either one of us wants each other for something real."

She spun away and went inside. The door shut with a slap that sounded as loud as a shot in the quiet dark.

Chapter Nine

Damn it, damn it, damn it.

Melanie had let Harris get to her. The dark night, quiet conversation and trip down memory lane had softened her heart toward him. Then he'd reminded her of the night they'd broken up and the devastation that had followed. She'd lashed out like a rattlesnake, and instead of finessing her way to an interview, she'd thrown their breakup—and her real reasons for getting close to him again—in his face.

She had headed up to her room, shut her door and sat there in the dark for a long time, thinking about her life and how it had turned out. Thinking about mistakes, lost chances, detours. Deep regrets.

It's like one day you woke up and changed into some-

one else. What happened to the risk-taking girl I fell in love with?

That girl had stood in her bathroom the day before they'd broken up, cramping and bleeding and realizing something had gone terribly, terribly wrong. It had taken losing her baby for Melanie Cooper to realize that all her bad, impetuous choices had led to the biggest failure she could imagine. A failure that had hurt someone she'd never get to meet. Maybe she hadn't caused the miscarriage by drinking too much at a keg party or racing into the icy ocean in just her underwear, but she also hadn't done anything to protect her baby, either, or to avoid a pregnancy by being more careful with birth control. She had vowed in that moment to change her life, to go to college and be more than the girl who broke the rules and got away with it.

She tossed and turned, then got up in the morning and started writing. She wrote up the story about Stone Gap's eldest resident on her computer, then emailed it to Saul. She grabbed a bite to eat in the kitchen, partly sad that Harris wasn't there, partly relieved, then went back up to her room, sat by the window and grabbed a brand-new legal pad and her favorite ballpoint pen.

She began to write, filling the pages of the crisp pad with words. The best way to get out of this town, away from Harris and all those memories, was to use her pen.

She started the story about the fire with finding the bear in the closet, that tender moment when Catherine had given the bear to her daughter and the two of them had hugged. Then she backtracked to the fire itself, leaving a blank space for what had started the blaze, since she hadn't been able to get that information from anyone she'd talked to. Maybe Colton Barlow, who was with the Stone Gap Fire Department, knew. He'd been one of the first on the scene. Later today she'd stop by the building project and see if she could talk to him.

She'd get the story, with or without Harris's help. And then she'd move on and away from him and everything he made her remember.

She got two and a half longhand pages written, then set the pad aside. Flexing those long-unused writing muscles had felt good.

Really good.

It was as if she was finding herself again by returning to the kind of writing that she loved. The stories that mattered, the stories that would touch people's hearts. Or would, if she got the rest of what she needed and could do it justice with her pen.

Crap. She'd gotten so tied up writing, she'd lost track of time. She had maybe ten minutes until she was supposed to pick up Ma and meet Abby at the dress fitting. Melanie left the notepad on the tiny desk in her room, then hurried out to her rental car and over to Abby's house. Her mother was waiting on the porch, her lips pursed and arms crossed over her chest.

Ma's gray trousers and coral sweater could have been the same ones Melanie remembered from childhood. Her mother found a style and stuck to it, pretty much 365 days a year, changing only the color. She probably had three dozen of those sweaters and just as many pairs of practical pants. Maybe it came from the years she'd worked as a receptionist at an insurance company, but her attire always seemed to scream *office*.

"About time." Her mother passed by Melanie and got into the passenger's side.

"Good morning to you, too, Ma." Melanie held the door while her mother climbed in the sedan, then came back to the driver's side and put the car in gear. The dress shop was only a couple of miles from Abby's house, which made for a quick car ride. "Abby texted and said she's running late, too. She got tied up at work."

"Well, if she organized her days better, she might be able to get out the door on time." Cynthia shook her head. "Neither one of you has any respect for a clock."

"Ma, Abby juggles more than you and me put together. Her boys are doing great, and she seems happy, so you really should lighten up." They were words Melanie had said a thousand times, but they never seemed to be heard.

"Because of those boys, it's even more important that she have everything on track. That's what I had to do when your father died and left me with two little girls to raise by myself." Ma settled her purse in her lap and folded her hands over the small leather bag. "At least you finally have your life in order. And I'm sure that when you and Adam have children, you will run your life on a schedule."

"I…I don't think we're going to have kids." Melanie parked in front of Daisy's Bridal Shop, put the car in Park and took the key out of the ignition.

Her mother put a hand on Melanie's arm before she

could get out of the car. "What? Why? He would make a wonderful father. Much better than that idiot Abby used to be married to."

Ma had never liked Keith, Abby's ex-husband—which Melanie understood, because she hadn't liked him much, either, given how he had left Abby and her children more than once. On the other hand, Adam, with his charm and good looks, had impressed her mother from the start. Maybe because he was on the cover of the magazines she saw in the checkout lane, or maybe because Adam had a natural schmoozing ability. Either way, Ma had seen him as the perfect son-in-law from the first day she met him. She'd never seen his faults—the self-centeredness, the undependability, the chauvinism.

Harris would have made a much better choice. Down-to-earth, smart, funny...

Masochistic thoughts. Harris had proved his disloyalty by breaking up with her without letting her tell him the truth. What guarantee did she have that he wouldn't do that again? Far better to put the man out of her mind.

"Let's go inside, Ma." Melanie got out of the car and avoided any more questions by holding open the door to the shop—which could double as Barbie's latest town house, given the decor. Poufy white chaise lounges peppered the pink carpeted floor and space between the mirrored pedestals. Dresses of every color hugged the racks against the walls. A small table in the center of the shop held champagne glasses and a tower of macarons.

Sweet. If she was going to have to stand around in a fancy dress and exchange small talk with her mother, having a little alcohol and sugar was going to make the whole ordeal much better. Or rather, a lot of alcohol.

The shop girl bustled up to them, holding two glasses of champagne. "Good morning! I'm Daisy. You must be Abby's family. Let's get you two started. You can put your things on the couch there, and while you try on your dresses, I'll keep everyone's glasses full of champagne. How does that sound?"

"Fantastic," Melanie said. Maybe a bit too quickly. Already, she was feeling the pressure of her mother's expectations pressing up against all the secrets she had hidden, the lies she had told. The fiction she had spun to avoid facing the truth.

For all her efforts to avoid risk and go down a different path, she had failed. Again.

"Great!" Daisy said. "Mom, you're in dressing room one, and sister, you're in dressing room two. I already hung your dresses inside. Call me if you need anything."

Melanie ducked into her dressing room and slipped into the teal-green dress she had ordered online. Abby had given her sister carte blanche on a dress, determined to keep the whole wedding as simple as possible. The dress had a sweetheart neckline and nipped in at Melanie's waist, giving her more curves than she showed in her usual jeans and T-shirts.

"Oh my, that is just beautiful!" Daisy said when Melanie stepped onto the main floor of the shop. "Come on, come on, stand up here." She took Melanie's hand and tugged her onto on the pedestals. "Just beautiful," she repeated.

Melanie would have to agree. The dress looked even better on than it had on the website. Ma came out of her dressing room, wearing a pale coral mother-of-the-bride dress. It had cap sleeves and a scoop neckline and ended just past Ma's knees. "Ma, that looks gorgeous."

Her mother shrugged, then got on the pedestal beside her daughter. "Abby picked it out."

Melanie sighed. What was her mother's issue with Abby, anyway? "I think it looks terrific. Abby has great taste."

"I agree!" Daisy said. "Now, I'm just going to duck in the back and grab some pins, just in case any of you need something nipped or tucked."

Melanie glanced at her reflection beside her mother's. Melanie stood slightly taller than her mother and had dark brown hair instead of blond. They had the same blue-green eyes that could edge toward either color, depending on the day. "Be happy for Abby, Ma. Dylan is a great guy, and I think he's going to be a great father for the boys."

"I *am* happy for her." Cynthia turned one way, then the other. "It's just…well, I always wanted the best for both of you. And you had your moments, but look at how you've turned out. Working for a national magazine. Living in New York City. Abby is living in this Podunk town and working a job that pays a third of what you make. I wanted more for her."

Daisy came breezing out, a pincushion in one hand. "All right. Let's nip and tuck where necessary." She stepped behind Ma first, pinning a dart into place above either hip. "Right here. And here."

"But Abby's happy," Melanie said. "Crazy happy. Isn't that enough?"

"When that man leaves her with those kids, happiness isn't going to pay the bills."

And there, Melanie realized, lay the crux of her mother's criticisms. Resentment of a man who had died before he could be a father, and a need to keep her daughters from ending up in the same boat, abandoned with children to raise.

"Dylan isn't going to do that, Ma. Abby made the right choice. It's not all about money."

"Try telling yourself that when you're working two jobs to put food on the table." Her mother shook her head. "You girls need to learn from my mistakes, not repeat them."

Daisy scooted over to Melanie. "Oh my. You should have ordered a size smaller. I'll have to take this in quite a bit." She gathered up the back of the dress and pinned down the spine.

There's an article idea—have your life fall apart and lose ten pounds quick and easy.

Melanie looked at her twin reflection with her mother and realized that she didn't want to become this jaded, unhappy woman. All the years she'd worked at the magazine, coupled with Adam's betrayal, had turned Melanie into someone who put up walls, kept others at arm's length. But unlike her mother, who pushed people away with an abrasive personality, Melanie kept everyone at a distance. If she opened up, she'd have to let everyone see what a colossal mess she'd made of her life.

"I need a few more pins," Daisy said. "I'll be right back."

Cynthia primped her hair and smoothed the front of the dress. "I hope Abby makes this one last. At least you and Adam have a life together. Now if you'd just have some children…"

"We aren't going to have children, Ma. We can't. Because…" When she'd been young, she'd lied to escape punishment, to gain approval, to smooth the waters in a rocky home. All those lies had piled up, turning Melanie's life into something she didn't even recognize. Someone she didn't want to be. She'd ended up going through the traumas of life alone—her miscarriage, her divorce, her job loss—instead of reaching out to the imperfect people who loved her.

The shop phone rang. Daisy answered it from the back of the store, her voice a low background murmur.

"Because why?" Ma asked.

Melanie swallowed and let the truth out. "Adam and I got divorced, Ma."

"You got…" Her mother's jaw dropped. She shook her head. "No, you didn't. You would have told me. And besides, you two were so happy. Why on earth would you get divorced?"

"We weren't happy. We hadn't been for a really long time. I'm not sure we ever were, really. I know you liked Adam—"

"He's a wonderful man." Her mother pivoted toward her on the dais. "One you should have appreciated."

"He was a jerk, Ma." Melanie sighed. How long had she kept that to herself? She hadn't even really told anyone at work. Adam was a darling of the modeling world, and that made him a star in the eyes of the magazine world, too. He charmed everyone he met, and the few times she did complain about him, her friends at the magazine waved off Melanie's concerns. By the time the divorce was final, Melanie had lost her job anyway, and it seemed easier to let the lie stand. "He cheated on me, pretty much the entire time we were married. I found out when he came home and told me he was in love with someone else. I filed for divorce the next day."

"When was this?"

"The divorce was final a year ago."

"A year ago!" Her mother glanced to the back of the shop, then lowered her voice. "Why would you keep that a secret from me for so long?"

Melanie opened her mouth to explain, then hesitated. A thousand things were wrapped up in the whys. Her childhood, her struggle to please someone unpleasable, the sense of failure she had battled most of her life.

Abby breezed into the store, saving Melanie from a response. "Hey, sorry I'm late. Wow, you guys look great. Those dresses are gorgeous!" She stopped by the pedestal. Her gaze flicked between Ma and Melanie. "Uh…did I miss something?"

"Your sister has just told me she has been divorced for a year." Ma put a fist on her hip and raised one judgmental brow. "I assume you knew about this and didn't say anything?"

"Ma, Abby didn't know anything. I didn't tell anyone."

Her mother kept talking, as if she hadn't even heard Melanie. "Why didn't you counsel her? Lord knows you've made that mistake yourself. You're the oldest. You should have—"

"Ma—"

"I had no idea Melanie's marriage was in trouble." Abby's gaze met Melanie's, and visible hurt flickered in her eyes. "She never told me."

The betrayal hung heavy in the bright pink room. Abby stood six feet away, but with the chill between them, it might as well have been six miles. Guilt filled Melanie's chest, burdened her shoulders. She'd never thought about how Abby would feel once she knew the truth—and realized how long Melanie had kept it from her. Melanie hadn't thought beyond her own need to keep pretending she hadn't failed. That she hadn't let them all down again.

In the end, she had done it anyway.

"You lied to me. Over and over again." The hurt in Abby's voice almost broke Melanie.

"I'm sorry." Two words that weren't nearly enough. But how could she tell them about how badly she'd needed to be a success in their eyes? About how she had left for college, determined to turn her life around, to become a better, more responsible person? To finally be someone they would all be proud of? And just when she had attained that, she lost it all, as if some cruel poltergeist had yanked the rug out from beneath her.

Daisy came out of the back room just then, her arms full of wedding dress. "Abby! You're just in time. I have your dress ready for you to try it on."

Abby flipped a glance at Melanie, then back at Daisy. "I'm sorry. I'm going to have to reschedule. I'm just not feeling up to a fitting right now." Then Abby walked out of the shop without ever looking back.

Swinging a hammer felt damned good. Harris wiped the sweat off his brow with the back of his hand, then reached into the coffee can beside him for a handful of nails. A few feet away, Jack Barlow was holding the other half of the wall they were framing. "I forget sometimes how hard this work is," Harris said.

"That's because you're the boss and spend your days telling other people how to build the houses, not doing the heavy lifting." Jack grinned. "Want me to finish up the wall?"

"No. I'm enjoying this. It feels…productive."

"That's why I love construction." Jack slipped the next two-by-four into place, then stepped back while Harris hammered it down. "All right. Now that this wall is in place, let's get the next one up. Before you know it, we're going to have a house."

And not a moment too soon, Harris thought. He glanced over at Catherine, who was handing out ice water and lemonade to the volunteers. John was cutting boards for the framing and handing them off to Luke Barlow. Dylan had picked up the Kingston kids and brought them to the community center for the afternoon. Vivian Hoffman at the Good Eatin' Café had donated sandwiches, and though there wasn't as big of a group here as there had been the first morning, all of the Barlow brothers had rotated in for at least part of the day. Della was busy drumming up support for the fund-raiser, which looked like it was going to be a big hit.

Except for one quick update visit, the television reporter had stayed away. Saul had talked to John a couple times about an interview, but John had asked the editor to respect the privacy of the family and Saul let it go. All in all, it was a good day. If not one that felt a tiny bit…empty.

He'd gotten up this morning, figuring he'd see Melanie at breakfast, but her rental car was already gone. He told himself that was good. She'd made it clear the other night that all she wanted was a story from him. Her words still stung, a slap that he hadn't seen coming. Of all the people he imagined trying to wheedle the truth out of him, Melanie Cooper wasn't even on the list.

"Looks like we have an extra set of hands," Jack said, nodding toward the driveway.

Harris turned and saw Mellie getting out of her car. God, she was beautiful. Her hair was back in a ponytail today, exposing the delicate lines of her neck. His gaze trailed down to the V of her T-shirt, over the curves of her breasts, her hips. Didn't matter how many years passed or how much the truth had hurt, his heart still skipped a beat whenever he saw her.

Damn, he was a masochist. He turned back to the wood and damned near took his thumb off when the hammer swung too wide and missed the nail head by a mile.

"Seems you're a bit distracted," Jack said. He chuckled. "A woman like that can drive you crazy."

"Who? Melanie? There's nothing between us. We're…"

"Friends?" Jack arched a brow. "Because it sure seems like a lot more than that by the look on your face. And the look on hers."

Harris saw nothing different from usual in Mellie's features. He picked up another nail. Sank it in place with one hard *thwap*. "We're just friends."

Maybe if he said it enough he'd believe it.

"If you ask me, a woman like that is the kind you shouldn't let get away," Jack said, leaning close to Harris. "I should know. I let Meri get away after high school and almost lost her before I got a second chance. Best decision I ever made."

"Some people just work out like that," Harris said. "But other relationships are…complicated."

"It's not complicated when you care about each other. I've seen you two together." Jack put his hands on his hips and stretched his back. "I'm feeling the need for a break. Let's get something to drink, then come back and finish this."

"Sure, sure." Harris put down the hammer so fast, it tumbled off the makeshift worktable and fell on the ground. He scrambled to put it in place, then brushed the sawdust off his jeans as he crossed to Mellie. Who was conveniently standing along the path to the water cooler, as if Jack had placed her there himself. Harris glanced at Jack, but the Barlow man was already heading in the opposite direction, a big grin on his face.

"You actually here to help? Or get the scoop?"

She scowled. "Why do you find it hard to believe I might be here just to help?"

"Because last time we spoke, you made it clear that all you want out of me is my story. And that's something I'm not giving you—or anyone."

"Let's call a truce, okay? I *am* here for a story, but today, it's just about the fund-raiser. I'm not as heartless as you think, Harris." She took a step closer to him. "You know me, or at least you used to. Have I ever been the kind of person who uses other people to get what I want?"

"That honor goes to my father." Harris studied her, pausing a beat to take in her heart-shaped face, the hint of a smile on her lips. Every inch of him ached to touch her, that masochistic urge pounding in his head along with an insidious voice saying that maybe she had just said that in the heat of the moment, but not really meant that all she wanted from him was the inside story on the fire. He put out a hand. "Truce."

She shook with him, then laughed. "Deal."

He reached for a pair of water bottles and handed her one, breaking their contact and changing the subject in one swift move. Every time he was close to her again, his thoughts got fuzzy and he forgot all those reasons why they weren't together. "I'm surprised at how quickly this is coming together. The Barlows have been a huge help."

"It's like this town is a team," she said. "Gives this jaded reporter a little hope that good people still exist in the world."

"They do indeed. This town has kind of grown on me." He'd spent several weeks in Stone Gap on this trip, long enough that Connecticut seemed farther away every day.

"Me, too, truth be told." She uncapped the water bottle and took a long drink. "I had a lot of fun writing that profile on the oldest resident for Saul. He liked it so much, he tried to talk me into taking over the paper so he can retire and fish all day."

If Mellie did that, she'd have to live in Stone Gap. Considering he was already thinking about moving here on a permanent basis, that meant they'd see each other more often. Harris wasn't sure if that was a good thing or a bad thing. "You know, if you were editor, you'd get to decide which stories were written. You could do more meaty pieces, or lighter stories. No more kale salad or thin thighs."

Mellie laughed. "Maybe Saul should put that in the job description."

Harris leaned against the tree and took a swig of water. The day shone bright and cheery, with a smattering of clouds in the sky and a light breeze. The hum of conversation carried in the air, punctuated by the pounding of hammers and the whine of a table saw. "I agree with you on the town. I've even been thinking about moving here permanently."

"Really? Why?"

"I have nothing holding me in Connecticut. I don't talk to my father, and my mother died last year. And I like it here. The people are fantastic." There was also enough custom home building in the surrounding areas to keep him busy. Maybe not commanding the prices he did up north, but the lower cost of living would counteract that. "Now, if I could just get Della's home cooking every day, I'd be all set."

She laughed. "It might be a little expensive living at the inn on a permanent basis, just to get home-cooked meals."

"I'd have to build a lot more houses, that's for sure." He tipped the water bottle in her direction. "What about you? Living here is a whole lot cheaper than living in New York. And that would mean you could afford to take on the assignments you like, if you didn't take over for Saul."

She scoffed. A tease lit her features. "Are you asking me to move in with you or something?"

The thought didn't totally terrify him. In fact, the idea of seeing Mellie every day seemed…nice. He tried to read her thoughts, but she was as cool as the breeze, and just as hard to pin down. He closed the gap between them. Her eyes widened, and the soft scent of her perfume filled the air. His gaze dropped to her lips. "Or something."

"Harris, this whole thing between us is temporary, nothing more than—"

To hell with caution, with past history. He leaned forward, scooped her into his arms and kissed her. She hesitated a moment, then her arms went around him, the water bottle cool against his back, and she kissed him. She fit against him as she always had, filling in the spaces inside him.

Mellie's kiss was tender and sweet, easing a gentleness out of him that spoke of long nights and dark spaces. He dropped his bottle to the ground, then cupped her face, deepening the kiss, bringing his body against hers. A mew escaped her, igniting a roar of desire inside him and shoving coherent thoughts out of his head.

The whir of a table saw jerked him back to the present moment. They were in a public place, and pretty damned far from any kind of a bed, even though every inch of him wanted to be in one with Mellie. Right now. And for the foreseeable future.

He grabbed at some sanity, stepped back and smiled down at Mellie. Her face was flushed, her breath hurried. "Temporary, maybe, but definitely more than just a thing."

She shook her head. "I'm going back to New York, Harris."

To his ears, the statement sounded less sure than the last time she'd said it. "Why don't we talk about how temporary this is over dinner tonight? Whether you stay here or go back to New York, it's just one meal."

She considered that for a moment. So long that he thought she was going to say no, but instead she nodded. "The Sea Shanty again?"

"I was thinking somewhere a little more private." He shifted nearer to her, keeping one hand on her waist.

Her eyes widened, and the flush bloomed in her cheeks. "Meet me in my room at seven?"

Mellie smiled, that seductive, sweet smile he knew as well as he knew his own name. "Are you cooking?"

"Not if I can talk Della into doing it." He moved closer, tamping down the urge to finish that kiss. "I promise, we'll have something edible. And memorable. Say yes, Mellie. Just say yes."

"You're a hard man to resist, Harris McCarthy."

"I'd say that works both ways, Melanie Cooper." He pressed one more quick kiss to her lips, then headed back to the job site.

Chapter Ten

The idea was insane.

This was only going to lead to a bad decision.

She should cancel.

Melanie picked up her phone at least a half a dozen times to text Harris and tell him they should catch dinner at the Sea Shanty again, or some other public place. Anywhere other than his room. Because being in his room, alone, meant...

Everything. Meant the attraction she'd been trying to pretend she no longer felt would go unchecked. There'd be a bed a few feet away, and after that kiss—

Well, being in bed with Harris had been a pretty frequent thought. She remembered what it was like to make love with a tender, considerate man like him. He'd learned her body, learned what she liked, and

every time they had sex was better than the time before. Was his memory of those things still good?

She took a shower, shaved her legs—telling herself
it was only because she wanted to, not because she was
thinking of Harris's hand running along her thighs—
curled her hair, then ignored her jeans and opted for
the single dress she'd brought with her. Simple and
cotton, the yellow V-neck dress skimmed her curves
and made her feel pretty.

Not that she cared about that, of course. She was
merely getting comfortable. Yup. That was all. She
was going to dinner tonight to get the inside scoop
on the fire, nothing more. A flicker of guilt reminded
her she'd told him she didn't use people to get what
she wanted—and here she was, doing that very thing.
Telling the story could be good, though, and a way to
help the family even more. Surely Harris could see
the logic in that.

She grabbed a bottle of wine she'd picked up at the
grocery store earlier, then headed down the hall. This
was crazy. Going on a date in a man's bedroom. Totally crazy. She should march back to her room, call
Harris and tell him she wasn't coming.

Except she didn't turn around. And didn't bail at
the last second.

He opened the door at her first knock. Because he
was as nervous as her? Standing right by the door, waiting for her? The thought sent a little thrill through her.

He grinned. "You're right on time. I have to admit,
I'm kinda surprised."

"That's one bad habit from high school that I broke

as an adult." She handed him the wine and tried not to look like an awkward teenager. All afternoon, she'd thought about that hella-hot kiss on the job site. How much she'd loved it. How much she wanted another. How much trouble that would bring in her life. Even now, the second she saw him, her pulse raced and desire coiled through her. "I hope you like red."

He ushered her in, then shut the door. The sound of the latch snicking into place sealed the decision to stay. He'd set up a small speaker beside his phone and the music segued into a love song, filling the air with a lazy, sensual beat. "Red's perfect. I don't care what wine we have. It's the company I've been looking forward to."

The room seemed to shrink in size. All she saw, all she was aware of, was Harris and his bed, just a few feet away. She caught the spicy scent of his cologne, felt the heat from his body. And forgot her own name. "So…uh, what's for dinner?"

Harris had pulled the room's small white desk away from the wall and secured a second chair from somewhere. Two covered plates sat on the desk, flanked by wine and water glasses, linen napkins, and polished silverware. Harris stepped away from her and lifted the silver covers. "Voilà. Della's chicken marsala with a side of mashed potatoes and roasted asparagus. Oh, and homemade biscuits, the best in the South, she says, and I believe her."

"Smells delicious." Her stomach rumbled and her mouth watered. Della was a damned good cook, and if the scents were any indication, it was going to be an amazing meal.

Harris pulled out one of the chairs, then made a sweeping gesture. "My lady?"

She laughed. Harris had always had a gallant side, which was one of the things she'd liked about him. All the other boys in high school had been awkward and self-centered, but Harris…he was different. Maybe it had been the wealthy upbringing, or some chivalry in his DNA, but whatever it was, she liked it. "If I knew this was a formal affair, I would have worn something fancier."

His gaze slid over her body when she approached the chair. "You look amazing, Mellie. Yellow looks good on you."

"Thank you." Her cheeks heated, and she broke eye contact. What was it about being alone with him that made her feel sixteen again? Shy and unsure, completely forgetting about the article she needed to write, the real reason she was here with him.

Alone.

In a bedroom.

With a bed mere steps away.

Harris opened the wine bottle—she'd bought a screw top, just in case he didn't have a corkscrew—and poured some into each of their glasses. She started to eat, so she wouldn't stare at his hands and think about them on her body. Except that didn't work very well, because her mind kept straying down that *bed is right over there* path.

"So you said Saul liked your article about the town's oldest living resident?" he asked.

Good. A work question. Maybe that would defuse

the desire in her body. "He did. He said he liked how I interviewed Evelyn's great-grandson and asked him what he thought she did to live so long. He said it added a nice punch of humor to the article." The praise from the small-town paper's editor had warmed Melanie more than she'd expected. It had been a long time since she'd written something with any kind of meat—not to mention, the first bit of strong editorial approval she'd gotten in a while. "It felt really good to turn that story in, I have to say."

Harris chewed a bite of chicken, then reached for the butter for his bread. "So, you never did tell me. What's the secret to living to a hundred and two?"

"According to Evelyn? Lots of whiskey and good sex."

Harris laughed so hard, he almost spit out his wine. "Really? That's a plan I can follow."

What was she doing? Bringing up drinking and sex, with a glass of wine in her and a bed just behind her? Was she flirting with him? Because this was getting her further away from her reason for being here, not closer.

Except right this second she didn't care about the article. Her career. Her life in New York. All she saw across from her was the man she had loved more than any other on the planet, his eyes soft and happy, and the past erased between them.

"Evelyn, uh, said she's been dating a younger man— he's ninety-eight—for some time now and that being with him is part of what keeps her young." Melanie took a bite of creamy, buttery mashed potatoes. They paired perfectly with the tender chicken marsala. Or so her taste buds said. Her brain had stopped functioning the minute she saw Harris smile.

"That's pretty incredible," Harris said, and the part of her that still cared what he thought was pleased he was impressed. They talked some more about her story as they ate, and the amazing meal Della had made began to disappear from their plates.

The wine was nearly gone, their plates almost clean, before Melanie circled the conversation back around to the fire. She almost didn't bring it up, because she wanted to hold on to these light, fun moments with Harris awhile longer. To go on thinking about that kiss, about his joke about them moving in together and about how much she had missed him in the years apart.

But in a week or so, she was going back to New York. To her apartment and her bills and her complete lack of a permanent job. She couldn't survive much longer on the little savings she had left. Reality had a nice way of smacking the dreaminess out of her head.

"The Kingstons are such a great family," Melanie said, sliding the sentence in as a natural segue from their conversation about the town. "I was really impressed with how they have pulled together with the community."

"They are great. One of those families who would give you the shirt off their back. Except now they need that shirt, and yet they are still giving back. Catherine baked cookies for the entire fire department, and John is giving all the volunteers free haircuts." The sun was almost done setting outside his window, casting a bright swath of gold across the room and off Harris's dark hair. She had fantasies of Greek gods for a second.

Focus on the article. On why you are here.

"Hopefully the article I'm writing about the fund-raiser will bring in more donations," she said. "And if I added one about the fire…you know, sort of laid out what happened—"

"No."

One word, succinct and clear. "But a little more publicity—"

"Just tell the bare minimum in the article about the fund-raiser, Mellie. Please. This family deserves their privacy. I thought I made that clear."

Maybe she could talk to Harris later, after the fund-raiser article ran, and change his mind. She couldn't understand why he wouldn't want as much publicity as possible, to help drum up the funds they needed. Surely Harris could see how that could change the lives of the Kingstons for the better. But that was a conversation for later, she decided, when he wasn't so sensitive to the subject.

She buttered another piece of bread, even though she was full. Maybe if she kept the words flowing between bites it wouldn't seem like so much of an interview? "How did you meet them? I mean, you weren't in town that long the first time, right?"

"When I was here before, I was working on a house for a baseball player who built just outside Stone Gap. I needed a haircut, and when I was driving through town on my way to the job site, I saw John's barbershop. I met him and his wife, and we hit it off. Then my mother died a few weeks later, and I…I was in a dark place for a while, and John was there for me."

"I'm so sorry about your mother, Harris. She was such a sweet woman."

"I felt so guilty when she died." Harris stared down at his plate, as if the words he was seeking were buried beneath his potatoes. He paused for a long time, while the faint sounds of children playing carried in on the breeze. "My father was hard on me, but he was horrible to her. She couldn't do anything right. She spent too much money on this, or went too cheap on that, or didn't say the right things at the dinner table. When I lived there, I tried to take on as much of the brunt of his anger as I could, but when I quit working for my dad, my father disowned me. It was a brutal argument, and I wanted nothing to do with him ever again."

Harris pushed his plate away and wrapped his hands around the stem of the wineglass. "Because of that I… I stayed away from my mom, too. I kept telling myself it was because he'd be furious if he found out she'd met with me and I didn't want her to pay the price for me striking out on my own, but it was really because I just couldn't deal with either one of them right then. Plus, I definitely didn't want to run into my dad and hear his diatribes again." He sighed, a heavy sound that spoke of deep regrets. "She was hurt and lonely, and though I talked to her often, she wanted me to visit. After I finished building the house down here, I promised to come see her. But she died before I could get home."

His mother was only in her fifties, if Melanie remembered right. She'd met Harris's mother a few times, when she'd stopped by his house to pick him up. His mother had been a slight, short, quiet woman, who clearly loved her son but rarely raised her voice above a whisper. The one encounter Melanie had had with Harris's father—after school one afternoon when he picked Harris up from detention—had shown him to be exactly as Harris described him: brutal. She couldn't imagine being married to a man like that, and frankly, Melanie was surprised Harris turned out so normal. That had to be his mother's influence. "Your mother was so young, though. What happened to her?"

"Lung cancer. She never told me about it. I think she didn't want me to worry." Harris shook his head and let out a curse. "If only I had gone home sooner…"

She covered his hand with her own, her thumb trailing across his wrist. "You couldn't have known, Harris."

"I should have gone home." He sighed. "I was a wreck after that, and John…well, he came and dragged me out of the bar and took me fishing, and talked to me until I got myself together. He took time off from the barbershop, time he couldn't afford, and he was just there for me as my friend. After what…"

Harris shook his head again. He pinched the space between his brows. "I owe him. More than I can ever repay."

After what… The words seemed to hint at something more, something Harris wasn't saying. Something he didn't want to say. There was a reason he kept resisting publicity on his heroism and generosity, a reason that seemed to go beyond being humble. "Did the fire department ever determine the cause of the fire?"

"They did."

Melanie waited, silent. She took her time eating the bread, stalling. If she left a wide enough gap in the conversation, Harris would fill it. Over the years, she'd learned that if she just stayed silent, people got uncomfortable with the silence and filled it with words.

What was she doing? Manipulating someone she cared about? This was no way to get a story. No way to restore her career. Before she could say *forget it, it's not important,* Harris filled the gap in the conversation.

"It was accidental," Harris said. The daylight was growing dimmer, casting shadows in the room. "A candle got knocked over."

"A candle did all that damage? Didn't someone see it burning?"

The speaker changed to a slow ballad from the '70s. Outside the window, there was the sound of children laughing, a horn honk, a lawn mower being shut down. The day was drawing to a close, and Stone Gap was settling down for the night.

"No one knew it was on the floor. When John knocked it over… What I'm telling you is not part of an article or a publicity piece or some fund-raiser promo. Is that clear?"

She nodded. "Of course."

Harris steepled his hands and drew in a deep breath. "He was too drunk to realize what had happened. John had gone home, already plastered and depressed, but realized he didn't want Catherine to see him like that again. He stumbled out of the house, and was getting into his truck to head back to the bar when the flames caught on the living room drapes."

John Kingston was drunk? That had to be why Harris had kept the story out of the media. Knowing Harris, he would protect his friend, and especially protect a family like that. One missed candle—and the Kingstons had almost lost everything. Except Harris—the Harris she had once been in love with and thought she would spend forever with—had been there and had saved them all. "How did you end up there at the right time?"

"John panicked. He called me, and before he even finished telling me what had happened, I was in my car. They don't live that far from the inn, so I was there in a few minutes. I called 9-1-1 on my way, but I drove so damned fast, I got there before the fire trucks did."

She could see it in her head—the dark night, Harris's calm strength, barreling through the deserted streets of Stone Gap. Him pulling into that driveway, racing out of his car, assessing the situation, making decisions. "And then you ran into the house to get the kids and Catherine? Why didn't John help?"

Harris shrugged, as if dashing into a house on fire was no big deal. "John…John was in no condition to do anything."

Her esteem for Harris skyrocketed. She had known and loved a high school boy, but the man he had become—smart, brave, strong—was someone she could very easily fall for. She met his gaze and saw fierce protectiveness there. He was a man, not a boy anymore, the kind of man a smart woman scooped up.

Unless that smart woman had a story to write. A career to save. A life to salvage. She tore her gaze away from him and focused on straightening her napkin on her lap. "I've met John. He doesn't strike me as an alcoholic."

"He had a bad day. I don't know what triggered it, but something reminded him of…" Harris drew in a deep breath, and when he released it, the air seemed to weigh a hundred pounds. "Of something that never should have happened."

She wanted to ease the worry in Harris's eyes, the hunch in his shoulders. Her hand snaked across the table to take his, but at the last second, she pulled it back. "That's awful. He must have terrible guilt about that night."

"He did, and he still does. He panicked when his family needed him most. But I know John, and I know if he'd been sober, he would have rushed into that house and carried them all out on his back. He's just a guy who got off track for a while. And…for good reason."

Hadn't Della said something about John losing his business? Melanie made a mental note to do some research tonight. Maybe that was what had depressed him that night. And the shame of being drunk enough to start the fire without noticing—not to mention, too drunk to save your own family—that was a good reason for Harris to want to protect the family from the press.

Thank God Harris was there. Harris, always the one to relate, to care, to give someone else a break. He was the complete opposite of his father, who was brutal and cold, chopping up businesses like they were melons. If the two men didn't look so much alike, she wouldn't have even thought they were related.

Damn. Why did Harris have to be such a good guy? Why did he have to care so much? And why did she feel this connection weaving between them again?

"I can relate to that, too," Melanie said softly. "The whole first part of my life was off track. And just when I thought I had it back on the right path..."

She let the words trail off. Finishing them would mean telling him about the miscarriage, the baby they'd almost had, the devastation that had made her shift and become more responsible and driven. The life they would have had together if that miscarriage never happened. It was too late for all that. Too late to start over. Too late to try again.

"Something came out of nowhere and knocked it off again," Harris filled in when she stopped talking. "I get that. But I think you've always had it together a lot more than you think." As if he'd read her mind, he took her hand, his touch warm and firm. "You're an amazing woman, Mellie. I've always thought that."

The touch added fuel to the desire already burning inside her. His fingers curled over hers, and in an instant, she was seventeen again and lying with Harris on a blanket under the stars. He'd held her hand up to the pale moonlight and traced her fingers with his own, sliding along her skin with slow, easy, practiced moves that were crazy erotic. They'd stayed there, making love over and over again, until the sun began to peek behind the trees and the town began to wake.

Harris's dark brown eyes met hers. She could have

looked away, could have gone back to her questions. Instead, she held his gaze, and when a question filled the space between them, she gave a small, short nod. Harris slid out of his chair, then took her other hand. She rose and stepped into his arms.

They began to dance, bodies moving in concert, stepping right, then left, back and forth, swaying closer and closer together with each step. The song on the radio was something by Norah Jones or Enya or someone like that. She couldn't have named the tune if someone paid her. Every one of her senses homed in on Harris, on the feel of his hand on the small of her back, the security of his opposite hand holding hers, and the way they brushed against each other from time to time. Every time her body hit Harris's, she noticed he had grown harder.

He lowered his mouth to hers and kissed her, slow, easy, tender. She stopped dancing and wrapped her arms around his neck, drawing him closer, deeper. She had missed him. Missed this. Missed being with a man who knew her body so well, he could have drawn a map of every hill and valley.

His hand slid between them, then over the top of her breast. She arched into the touch, cursing the clothes she wore, the slight distance they created between her skin and his touch. With one finger, he pushed the neckline of her dress to the left, then danced his fingers inside, under the lacy cup of her bra and over her breast.

When he grazed her nipple, she gasped. It was like setting off a ten-ton bomb in her midsection. All she wanted was more. Now. Right now.

Melanie pressed her pelvis to his, and there was no mistaking he wanted the same thing. "Harris," she whispered, because she couldn't think of another single thing to say.

"I have missed you, Mellie," he whispered against her lips. "Missed touching you."

"I've missed that, too." Her eyes watered, and the words caught in her throat. Melanie Cooper, who rarely betrayed an emotion or lost her cool, was falling hard for Harris McCarthy all over again.

"I want you," he said, "but only if you want this, too. We both know this isn't anything perm—"

"I don't care, Harris. I really don't. Right now, right here, please...please don't make me wait anymore."

That was all he needed. He reached behind her, slid down the zipper of her dress, then nudged it off her shoulders. She stepped back and let the fabric tumble to the floor with a whisper. Harris's gaze took in her lacy pale pink bra and panties, and a smile curved across his face. "Good Lord, you are beautiful."

She stepped forward and undid the buttons of his shirt one at a time, revealing inch after inch of his muscular chest. She parted the cotton panels, then slid the shirt down his arms. In the years they'd been apart, Harris had grown taller, broader, more muscular. She danced her touch along the ridges of his abdomen, over the contours of his biceps.

He dipped his head to kiss her neck, and she nearly came undone. Harris trailed kisses along her neck, down the valley of her breasts, while he undid the clasp and let the lacy fabric drop. He kissed her breast, then took one nipple in his mouth and sucked gently.

An inferno of desire erupted in her. She didn't want to wait, didn't care about taking their time. She grabbed his hand, stepping backward until she hit the bed. They tumbled onto the mattress, then rolled over and between each other, shedding Harris's pants, his briefs, her panties.

Then they were naked and sliding along each other's bodies, coming closer and closer to him entering her. She knew how that would feel, knew the bliss that would sink into her with him. And knew that after this, she'd want him even more. She was playing with fire, and right now, Melanie didn't care.

Harris grabbed a condom out of his wallet and slid it on. He braced himself over her, holding her gaze again for one long second. She surged up, grabbing him in a "stop hesitating" kiss, and he plunged into her.

She arched on the bed, then grabbed his back as he slid in and out of her in practiced strokes that somehow managed to hit every single nerve ending inside her. Harris hadn't forgotten a thing. Not a single damned thing.

And when those strokes multiplied and the heat inside her built, and she came, gasping his name, clawing at his back, she thought how damned grateful she was that Harris McCarthy had a good memory.

Chapter Eleven

Harris lay in his bed with Mellie in his arms, her head on his chest, the sweet scent of her perfume filling the air between them, the moment as fragile as a china teacup and ten times more beautiful. He was almost afraid to move, lest she remember she'd vowed this was only a fling.

He understood that. When they'd been young and getting married seemed like something only old people did, he had let her go at the first hint of trouble, instead of sticking it out and working things out. But now, with the passage of time and the learning of lessons about the shortness of life, Harris didn't want to let her go so easily again. He'd made a mistake that night they broke up, making assumptions and accusing her without letting her explain her side. He wouldn't be a fool again.

They had a little over a week left here before she went back to New York. He hoped it would be enough time.

Because tonight, Harris had realized he had never stopped loving Mellie. And if there was a chance in hell, he was going to do his best to get her back.

Melanie sneaked back to her room around three in the morning, careful not to wake Harris. All those feelings of reminiscing and missing had been replaced with a flashing neon sign in her head:

Big mistake.

What had she been thinking? She'd wanted to maintain distance, not close it. The guilt she'd been feeling about not telling Harris her real reasons for getting entangled with him tonight had quadrupled.

She had thought about waking him up and pleading her case about the article again. In the end, she'd decided to write the article first, show it to him and let him see that her intentions were good. That she wasn't out to exploit the Kingstons like that TV crew—she truly wanted to help them, too. She would include information about the fund-raising efforts, and if the article got picked up nationwide, it could mean a windfall for the family.

Melanie sat down at her desk and began to write, scrawling across the legal pad as fast as her hand could move, filling in where she had left off before, fleshing it out, deepening the emotion. The story was a good one, and even as she berated herself again for sleeping with Harris last night, the more the words flowed, the happier she felt. She wrote about the candle falling, how one simple mistake had had a domino effect that changed so many lives. And then she wrote about how one man was setting out to reverse those changes and bring a family back together.

When she was done, she skimmed the handwritten pages of the legal pad. Right now, there wasn't a thing she wanted to change. She'd let it sit for a day or so and then run it by Harris before she typed it into the computer and sent it to Saul. Maybe ask him if it was okay to pitch the story to some national outlets, too.

As dawn began to break, she remembered the information about John losing his company. Maybe she should include that, too—and maybe it would help increase business at the barbershop. People could understand someone who was down on their luck, who'd lost everything more than once and needed some help to get back on his feet.

It took some determined googling, but a half hour later, Melanie hit on what she had been looking for. And when she saw a set of three very familiar letters in the headline of Local Machining Company Shuttered, she knew why Harris had kept the truth from her.

And why he had lied last night.

All the sweet emotion she'd felt in his arms disappeared. Harris hadn't told her the truth—and she was pretty damned sure he hadn't told John, either. The Kingstons were unlikely to be so kind to him if they knew he was part of the reason their business had been shut down.

The clock ticked past nine. Melanie picked up her phone and made a couple calls, then took out her pen and added another paragraph. One that hurt her heart, and told her that the Harris who had broken up with her at eighteen was the same man today that he'd been then. Only a fool didn't learn her lesson.

She got dressed and headed out of the inn, hurrying past the kitchen in case Harris was up and eating breakfast. She'd made her mistake by sleeping with him. She wasn't going to compound it by seeing him again. No, she had her story. She didn't need anything from him ever again.

Della and her sons were busy on the lawn of the inn, setting up for the fund-raiser tomorrow. They'd hung streamers from the deck and placed small tables on the thick grass. One long table at the back would hold silent auction items, and Jack Barlow was building a small stage for a local band to play on.

Melanie gave the Barlows a wave. If she stayed and talked to them, chances were good that Harris would make an appearance. She'd cover the fund-raiser tomorrow, slip in and out for only as long as she needed to get enough for her article, and avoid him.

And avoid what sleeping with him had awakened in her heart. Because her heart sure as hell wasn't listening to her mind. No, her foolish heart was back in high school, all in love and imagining a forever future with Harris.

Losing the baby had broken that dream. And when Harris thought she was cheating—and instead of being there to hold her and console her, he'd accused her and left—the broken pieces of the dream had shattered beyond repair. Ironic that he was the one hiding the truth today when that used to be her specialty.

Until now. Until everything got more complicated, and Melanie got tired of covering her tracks. And avoiding the truth.

She'd start with heading over to see Abby. After the other day, she wasn't so sure Abby would talk to her, but she couldn't leave this crevasse between them.

Her sister was just coming down the porch stairs when Melanie pulled in. The boys weren't home— probably at school—and Melanie could see Ma inside the still-open front door, gathering up her purse. "What are you doing here?" Abby asked.

Melanie took a few steps closer, shading her eyes against the sun. "I don't want to leave it like this, Abs. Look, I'm sorry I lied to you."

Abby threw up her hands. "You've done it all your life, Melanie. And every single time, I've covered for you. I kept thinking that one day, you'd grow up and get honest with yourself, with the people who love you. When you got that job and married Adam, I thought you finally had." She shook her head. "But nothing's changed."

"Everything has changed. *I've* changed."

Abby arched a brow.

"I have," Melanie insisted. But then she paused. Had she really? She thought of Abby's words, and wondered if she was lying to herself now, too. She hadn't been honest with Harris, not about the past, and not about the present. She had kept the truth about the status of her job and her marriage from her family. No one knew about the miscarriage and how that had devastated her. Maybe it was time to be more honest, by starting with being more present. "I want to help with the wedding, Abby. That's why I'm here. You have to visit the florist today, right? And talk to the new caterer?"

"I can do that with Ma." If anything said *I don't want you around*, choosing their mother for a shopping buddy did. Abby dug her keys out of her purse and unlocked her car. "I've got to go."

"Abby—"

But her sister brushed past her and climbed into her car, then shut the door. A second later, Ma came down the stairs. "Your sister is very angry with you," she said.

"I got that." Melanie let out a huff of frustration. She'd hoped this would go differently.

"I have no idea why you would keep a secret like that," Ma said.

"Really? When all you've ever done is judge and criticize us?" Melanie shook her head. "I've done exactly one thing that you ever approved of, and that was marrying Adam. I can't imagine why I'd sugarcoat the truth about the end of my marriage."

"That was more than sugarcoating, Melanie. That was full-on lying." Her mother pursed her lips, then softened. "I am too critical of you girls. I just…I wanted more for you both than I had. It was never meant to hurt you."

It was probably as close to an apology as Melanie would ever get from her mother. "I was wrong for lying. I didn't want to disappoint you or Abby, and I just kept thinking… I kept thinking I'd fix it all somehow and then it wouldn't be a lie anymore when I said everything was fine."

"And now you've gone and ruined your sister's wedding." Ma flicked a glance at the car. "Maybe it's about time you started thinking about other people first, and the ramifications of what you say—or write."

Her mother got in the car, and Abby backed out, driving over the grass to get past Melanie's car. The two of them were gone a second later, leaving Melanie in the driveway. Alone.

The sound of an incoming text jerked Harris out of sleep. As he reached for the cell, he realized the bed was empty. Mellie was gone. Her pillow still held the impression of her head, but the sheets were cold. He checked his phone—no message from her. She'd sneaked out, without a word.

He scrolled down to the new message. Meet me at the café in an hour, John had written. Nothing more. Harris replied with a yes, then got ready. The curtness of John's text was odd. Very odd.

An hour later, Harris was sitting at a back booth in the Good Eatin' Café, a cup of coffee growing cold before him. John swung in a few minutes late, nodding to people as he passed them before dropping into the booth across from Harris.

John was a thin man, going prematurely bald. He had a two-day scruff of beard on his face, and he'd lost about ten pounds, but his eyes were clear and cold. He took off his ball cap and set it before him. "I thought you were my friend."

"I was. I am." A stone sank in Harris's gut. He knew, before John spoke, what the other man was going to say. How it would change everything.

"Why is the man who put me out of business so eager to build me a new house? You feeling guilty about what you did?"

Harris let out a long breath. He waved off the waitress. "Yeah. Very much so."

"You were the one who called my CFO and told him we were losing the contract with the truck manufacturer."

"Yes."

"And you knew that us losing that contract would also take away ninety-five percent of our business and annual revenues."

"Yes."

"And that I would have to lay off every single person in my company. Watch the women cry and the men beg, and hear these families suffer when their unemployment ran out or the new competitor you put in our place wouldn't hire them?"

"It wasn't…" Harris sighed. "Yes."

"The new manufacturer actually charged more. Did you know that? In the end, it *cost* that automotive plant money to put us out of business. All those people lost their jobs. For what? For nothing. For you and your father to pad your wallets with a kickback from a family friend who wanted an in with the automotive industry and do a favor for some client."

"I was simply doing what I was told." Except Harris

could have refused. But he knew that in the end, his father would have had someone else ruin John's business.

"What am I now? Some charity case you can take on?"

"No. You're my penance." Harris folded his hands and leaned forward. "I worked for my father for a couple years. It was the worst two years of my life. I thought if I did everything he asked me to do, he would be proud of me. He'd see that I was smart and capable. And he'd listen to my thoughts. Instead, he sent me out to do his dirty work. I shut down more companies than just yours, John. And every time, I felt horrible. But yours…" Harris shook his head. "I sat in my office for an hour that day before I made the call, looking at the pictures from the company picnic."

John nodded. "We had those on our website. Potluck, horseshoe games, even a potato sack race. Employees loved it."

"And I thought to myself, what am I doing? Why am I doing this? Why am I following the orders of a man I can't stand?"

"Yet you did it."

"In the end, I did. I called your CFO and delivered the news that you had lost the contract and were never getting it back. I ended up giving my notice to my father a few days later. Then, once I made some money from my building business, I started trying to find the people who were still down on their luck because of my father's decisions, and my mistake in implementing them." Harris ran a hand through his hair. The waitress nodded in their direction, but he shook his head. "I'm not going to make excuses. It was wrong. I was wrong. And all I've been trying to do ever since is make it right."

John considered this information for a while. He watched a couple stroll by outside, his gaze far from the table. "Do you know what happened that night? Why I was so drunk?"

"The night of the fire?" Harris shook his head. "No."

John swiveled back to look at Harris. All the hurt and outrage shone in his eyes. "One of my former employees called me. She was desperate for a job, and was hoping I could help her. They'd lost their car, their home, had to pull their son out of college and go live in some crappy apartment in a cramped building. And you know what? I had nothing to give her. No advice. No help. I looked around at my house, a house we were on the verge of losing to foreclosure, and thought I had failed my employees, and more, failed my own family. My kids were going to lose everything, and we were going to end up like my employee, in some one-bedroom apartment in the city while I tried to find some kind of place that would employ a man in his forties who didn't have much on his résumé besides a failed company and a few haircuts. I started drinking and kept right on drinking, because I was pissed and full of guilt and depressed about the whole thing. I never even noticed the candle." He lifted his gaze now, his eyes filled with sorrow, not outrage. "But you were there, in an instant after the fire started."

Of all the people he had helped, no one had figured it out. They'd all thought of Harris as a nice guy, helpful, maybe a little generous with his time. He'd helped them all anonymously, and taken his satisfaction in the smiles on their faces. But the time for hiding the truth about his father, about Harris's responsibility in all this, was over, consequences be damned. "When you called me that night, you were a mess. I just knew something had happened. I rushed over there and when I saw the flames…" Harris shrugged, a simple gesture that didn't begin to cover for that horrifying moment when he'd thought the Kingstons were dead. "I'm glad I was there."

"I don't want you to think for a moment that I'm not grateful for you saving my family," John said. "I am. And for all you're doing now. But I don't want to be your charity case."

"You're not. You *are* my friend, you really are." Harris fiddled with the place mat. "I even felt guilty about that, you know? My mother died, and I was a wreck, and there you are, the man I put out of business, dragging me out of a bar and setting me straight. You told me something that night that has stayed with me."

"Me? I had some wisdom?" John scoffed. "My wife will disagree."

Harris chuckled. "Catherine thinks the sun rises on your head, and you know it. You told me once that feeling guilty about the past doesn't make anything better. All it does is make the present miserable. The best thing to do is to be here now, for the people who love you and need you, and let the rest take care of itself."

John turned his baseball cap around and around in his hands for a long moment. He stared down at the red bill, the image of the Cardinals on the front. "And that's what you've been doing with me and my family."

"Trying to."

"All right then." John plopped the cap on his head. "I don't like what you did to my company, but I am beyond grateful for what you did for my family. And if it's not too much to ask, I have a few former employees who could use some work. Maybe they could come hang some Sheetrock or something."

Harris thought about this for a moment, then nodded. "They'll need some training, of course, but if they worked for you, I'm sure they were great employees, who would work hard. If I can't hire them all, I'll find people who can. I wish I could do more."

"You saved my life and my family. I'd say that makes us square." John slid out of the booth and got to his feet.

"Before you go…how did you find out about all this?"

John shrugged. "Some reporter called me this morning. Asked a few questions, and I put it together. Her name sounded familiar. I think I met her, out at the site. Melanie something?"

Harris knew exactly who John meant. The one woman he thought he could trust. Turns out he'd been wrong. Again.

The fund-raiser was in full swing by the time Melanie arrived, notepad in hand. The band was the same one she'd heard at the Comeback Bar that first night, which made her think of Harris. And miss him, damn it.

She'd had time to think about his connection to John Kingston over the last day or so. The shock had subsided, and with it, the anger that he hadn't told her earlier. Once she gave herself some time to process—and put the pieces together—she'd realized that the pot who had told lies for a living had no business calling the kettle anything.

The fund-raiser was already busy, a good sign for the target financial goal. There were games for the kids—cornhole, lawn darts, a bounce house—and several tables of food and silent auction items. From what Melanie could see, most of the town had shown up. Saul was standing behind one of the food tables, handing out pretzels.

The editor smiled when she approached. "Well, hello, Melanie." He took a five-dollar bill from a teenager and exchanged it for a pretzel. "How's my favorite writer?"

"Great. I'm just about done getting what I need for the story on the fund-raiser. And, if you're still interested, I have enough to write an article on what happened the night of the fire. I was going to type it up tonight and send it over to you."

Saul's eyes widened. He turned away from the pretzels and lowered his voice. "You got Harris to talk to you? I hear he wouldn't even talk to the TV people. He just kept saying the family had no comment and wanted the media to respect their privacy."

That wave of guilt hit her again. She had yet to tell Harris that she had written the story, that she was intending to have it published. "I interviewed Catherine Kingston, Colton Barlow and some of the people at the building event. Even got a couple quotes from

John. Harris was more reluctant to talk to me, but he did. Some."

She had to tell Harris the truth before Saul printed the piece. He'd be mad, but she was sure that the media attention would bring in even more donations, which was a good thing. Surely he would see that and understand. The article she'd written had been fair, but honest.

"Great! I'll run it with the recap of the fund-raiser in the paper that comes out on Tuesday."

Tuesday? That was only three days away. She wanted to tell Saul no, that she wasn't going to be ready by then.

Because she wasn't ready to tell Harris. The second she did, she risked him walking out of her life forever. And maybe that was the real reason she had stayed silent all this time—

Because she was falling for Harris McCarthy all over again. Any hope of a future with him meant being honest—about the past and the present.

Saul handed out another pretzel and put the money into the cash box on the table. "Are you sure I can't talk you into a permanent position? Maybe co-editor on a part-time basis to start? If I retire entirely, I might go crazy. A man can only spend so many hours fishing."

A permanent position meant staying in Stone Gap. Giving up her life in New York and living here with her sister and her nephews. And Harris, if he did settle in this town.

"I appreciate the offer, Saul, but—"

He put up a hand. "Think about it. Stone Gap takes time to grow on some people. Give it another week, then come talk to me."

She agreed, bought a pretzel and walked away. As she wandered around the event, she talked to a few more residents, getting quotes to fill out her article, with tidbits about why they were supporting the fund-raiser, how well they knew the Kingstons and how the town had come together. The more people she talked to who raved about Stone Gap, the more she wondered if maybe she could be happy here.

She loved New York—the busyness of it, the buildings, the constant motion. But she didn't have a community there, not like they had here. She had neighbors, most of whom she only knew in passing. If her apartment burned down tomorrow, she couldn't imagine the people on her block—never mind her neighborhood—doing anything more than offering some sympathy.

Across the lawn, she saw Harris talking to Jack Barlow. Jack Barlow was a good-looking man, with a short military-style haircut, a defined body and a ready smile. But Harris—

He was the one who made her heart skip. Damn it.

She started to turn away—procrastinating yet again on what she needed to do—when Harris noticed her, said something to Jack, then crossed toward her. She should have left, should have gone and interviewed someone else, should have done anything other than wait, but she was rooted to the spot, watching his long stride bring him closer and closer.

"You left in the middle of the night."

Damn. He got right to the point. "I had some work to do."

"And didn't say anything to me." A group of kids ran

by with giant wands in their hands that trailed looping iridescent oval bubbles. "Why?"

"We both knew this was temporary." Which wasn't really an answer, but there was a storm brewing in Harris's eyes and her good intentions wavered.

"Temporary as in over now that you got your story?"

Melanie's stomach plummeted. "It wasn't about that."

"You called John and told him I was the one who put him out of business. Was it worth whatever you're going to get paid?" He shook his head. "I can't trust you. I couldn't back then, and I clearly can't now, either."

"There's the Harris I remember. Jump to conclusions before you get your answers." She cursed under her breath. "You've always been so willing to believe the worst about me, instead of giving me a chance to explain. What are you so afraid of?"

"Me? I'm not afraid. You're the one who runs as soon as things get too difficult. Whether it's to someone else or back to the city."

"You still think that night was about someone else, don't you?" She shook her head. "You couldn't be more wrong, Harris, if you tried. You know, I get it that your father wasn't a man you could trust. He hurt you, hurt your mother, hurt the people whose businesses he closed. I think that turned you into someone who thinks everyone is going to hurt you. But I'm not that person. I never was."

"Then what were you doing there that night, in the arms of another man?"

"Being comforted. Because you weren't there. Because you couldn't wait long enough for me to explain anything. Dave was a friend from that job I had after school, the one at the pizza place. He just happened to be there when I…when the worst thing in my life happened to me."

Confusion filled his eyes. "What are you talking about?"

"Does it even matter anymore?" She sighed. "You already see me as the enemy, as someone who used you to climb the career ladder. Because that's a whole lot easier than opening up your heart and trusting someone, isn't it?"

"Or telling the truth. I'm not the only one who has trouble trusting other people."

"You're right." She thought of all the damaged relationships in her wake, the people she had pushed away because it was easier than admitting she had failed. "Trust has never come easily for me. Maybe it's all about my mother's constant criticism or my dad dying when I was a baby, or maybe I'm just more jaded than other people. It doesn't matter. Because I'm tired of carrying around all these lies and mistakes. I want what Abby has. What the Barlows have. I want family and friends and love."

"There's your headline for tomorrow's paper. Be sure to run it beside an article about how Harris Mc-Carthy broke your heart again." He shook his head. "Goodbye, Melanie."

He turned on his heel and strode away. Melanie watched him go and told herself her heart wasn't shattering. That she didn't care. She was going back to New York, and she was going to get over Harris McCarthy.

All over again.

A few minutes later, Melanie made up an excuse to leave the fund-raiser. She drove around Stone Gap for a long time, watching neighbors greet each other with a friendly wave, the postman making deliveries and chatting with a customer, a family of four walking a puppy to the park. It was all so wholesome and perfect and...

Exactly the kind of life she had thought she hated when she was young. The small town in Connecticut had felt stifling with the expectations of the people around her, the rules and restrictions. She had rebelled every chance she got, and then moved to a world as different from that as night from day.

And where had she ended up? Right back in a small town, with rules and expectations—but this time, she viewed it all from a very different perspective, especially when it came to good people who seemed to be living very happy lives.

It was time to stop running, she decided. To start facing the consequences of her decisions. To go after what she had always wanted and never dared to hope for.

Melanie pulled over, sent a text, then started driving again. She had pulled into a parking space before she heard the ding of an answer. One word: Okay.

Consequence number one, about to be faced.

She turned off the car, then got out and walked into the Good Eatin' Café, which, judging by the scents when she opened the glass door, fit its name. A gray-haired woman bustled forward, arms out, as if she were about to hug Melanie. "Welcome, welcome! I'm Miss Viv, the owner of the Good Eatin' Café. Table or booth?"

"A booth would be great, thank you."

"You got it." Viv gave her a smile, then led her to a booth and handed her a menu. "Our home fries won a blue ribbon at the state fair last year, but if you ask me, the best thing on the menu is the coconut cream pie. Also a blue-ribbon winner, and absolutely perfect as any meal, not just dessert."

Melanie liked Viv immediately. She was gregarious without being pushy and had that same friendly air about her that seemed to be part of every resident of Stone Gap. "I'll keep that in mind. Thank you, Miss Viv." She ordered a coffee, then sat down to wait.

The diner was cute, with a long counter dotted with red leather swivel stools. A display stand held sugar-dusted doughnuts beside the cash register, tempting every customer with one last treat as they paid. A burly man in a white apron hustled around the kitchen, greeting Viv as she came in and poured the coffee.

The radio was playing oldies, songs from the '70s that made Melanie think of summer afternoons at her grandmother's house. The diner wasn't too busy, with only a handful of filled tables and a couple of the bar stools occupied. She recognized a couple familiar faces from the building project yesterday and from the fundraiser earlier, but didn't remember anyone's name. Still, people gave her friendly nods and small waves of recognition. Since most people in town were still at the fund-raiser, business at the café was light today. Melanie had been counting on that when she sent the text.

The door to the diner opened, and her sister entered. Abby stood in the doorway, looking unsure, as if she was going to turn around and leave at any second. Melanie rose and waved toward her table.

"I have a lot to do today," Abby said as she sat down. Her features were icy, her voice devoid of emotion. "I'm not staying long."

"I just want to talk, Abs."

Abby sat back against the vinyl seat. "So talk. Start with telling me why you have lied to me a hundred times over the last year about you and Adam."

Melanie fingered the edge of the menu. "That's not the only thing I lied about."

Abby didn't say a word. The air between them chilled even more.

"I lost my job at the magazine last year, too," Melanie said.

"Why wouldn't you tell me? We talk all the time, Melanie. And all you've been doing is lying to me, every single conversation."

"I lied because I was embarrassed. At first, when I lost my job, I thought I'd find another one right away. When I didn't, so much time had gone by that I thought if I told you the truth, you would be mad at me for lying."

"I *am* mad at you for lying." Abby shook her head, then let out a breath. "You know what? I'm not mad. I'm hurt and disappointed. When you were fifteen, I could write this kind of thing off as you being a teenager and my wild little sister. But you're twenty-nine, almost thirty, Mel. When are you going to get your life together?"

"My life is together. Or…it will be." Melanie paused when the waitress dropped off her coffee. Both Abby and Melanie waved off the idea of food. "I got off track—"

"Again."

"Hey, I'm not stealing from the corner market. And I'm not breaking into the school to go skinny-dipping. I got divorced and I lost my job. Those are normal, adult things." Melanie cupped the hot mug of coffee and stared into the dark, rich brew. "But you're right. It's all tied back to the same thing. I've never felt like I could live up to your example, Abs. You were the smart one, the one who had it together, the one who knew what she wanted to do and who she wanted to be. And no matter what I did, it seemed like Ma…" Tears threatened behind her eyes, choked her voice. "Never saw me as anything other than the kid who screws up everything."

Abby's features softened. "Oh, Mel, that isn't about you. It's about her. Ma, for whatever reason, isn't happy with her life. Maybe she thinks complaining and criticizing will make things better. I don't know."

Melanie fingered the edge of her place mat. "You're probably right. And even if I had told her about the divorce and my job, she would have found something I did wrong with that, too."

"She does the same thing with me. I get that." Abby thanked the waitress for her coffee, then reached for a pair of sugar packets. She tore off the tops and sprinkled sugar into her cup. "Why didn't you come to me? I'm divorced. I've lost jobs before. I would have understood."

Those damned tears kept on brimming in her eyes, blurring her vision. "You were so proud of me when I got my degree and got married, then got a job. You kept going on and on about how awesome I was doing, and when things all fell apart, I just didn't want to see that look in your eyes again."

"What look?"

Melanie motioned toward her sister. "*That* one. The one that says, *what'd you screw up this time, Melanie?*"

"I wouldn't say that. I've never said that."

"No, you never have," Melanie admitted. In all those years, Abby had never criticized her little sister. She'd offered gentle advice and encouragement and lots of hugs. "You've always helped me out and given me advice and loved me. But it was in your face. That look like you were disappointed in me."

"Melanie, you are smart and confident and ten times stronger than me. I've never been disappointed in you. If anything, I was…envious."

"Envious? Of me? Why?" The waitress started to approach, and Melanie waved her off.

Abby's face softened. "You, my little sister, had the guts to break the rules. To step out of the box. I got married right out of high school, had kids and the house in the suburbs. I got married so young, I felt like I never lived. Never got to do any of the fun things you did."

"You were my hero, Abby," Melanie said. "The one who was there for me when Ma was hard on me, or I got upset about Dad. You were—and are—such a good mother and a great role model. I idolized you when I was growing up and missed you so much when you married Keith and moved out. Half the reason I acted up was because I figured I could never be as good as you, so I might as well go the opposite direction."

"All these years, the two of us envied each other and never said anything."

Melanie shrugged. "True."

"That's kind of crazy." Abby shook her head. "And this whole fight is kind of crazy."

The words brought a rush of relief and gratitude to Melanie's heart. The tears she'd struggled to hold back spilled over and down her cheeks. She reached across the table and grabbed her sister's hands. "It is. I'm so sorry, Abs. I really am."

"I totally forgive you. If you'll still be my maid of honor."

"Of course. I already got the dress."

Abby laughed, then slid out of the booth the same time as Melanie. The two of them embraced in a long, tight hug. They didn't care about the stares of the other diners or the coffee growing cold. They cried on each other's shoulders and mended years of wounds.

"This is an occasion that calls for two slices of pie," Viv said. She smiled at Melanie and Abby. "On the house."

Chapter Twelve

Harris headed inside the inn a little after seven. The fund-raiser had surpassed its goal, giving the Kingstons a little breathing room on top of everything they needed to finish filling the new house. John had beamed like a man who'd just won the lottery, with his kids by his side and Catherine snuggled up against his chest.

A part of Harris envied him. A man who had a family, a woman he loved and a second chance to be the man he wanted to be with both of them. The road ahead for John and his family would have bumps and detours, but Harris was sure they would make it work. Seeing and hearing the commitment in John, and the deep love in Catherine's face, meant this was going to be a happy ending, and for the first time since he'd made that call to John's CFO, Harris could sleep at night.

As for Melanie—he ignored the ache in his chest. It would go away. Someday.

Della was sitting at the kitchen table, tallying up receipts when Harris walked in with the last load of tablecloths and dishes from the fund-raiser. "Oh, thank you, Harris. But really, you're a guest and you shouldn't be doing that."

"I don't mind at all. I can't believe how successful it was." Della and her family had gone above and beyond in setting up and hosting the event. The Barlows were a popular family in town, which had drawn in people who didn't know the Kingstons but wanted to get behind a good cause. Such a contrast to the town where he'd grown up and the love/hate relationship most people there had with his father. Harris was pretty sure that if his father was on fire, there were a lot of people who would stoke the flames instead of putting them out.

Della smiled. "I'm not surprised. Stone Gap will always rally around one of its own."

"I didn't think places like this still existed." He pulled out a chair and sat across from her. The entire day had been wonderful and warm, infused with a giving, welcoming community spirit. He had only been to Stone Gap twice, and yet every resident greeted him like he'd lived here all his life. "I really like it here. It's a wonderful place to live."

Della cocked her head and studied him. "Does that mean you're thinking of making it a permanent stay?"

"I am. But…"

"It all depends on what happens with someone else who is staying at this inn?" Della laughed at Harris's surprise. "I've seen the way you two look at each other. When you asked me to send up a private dinner for two, it didn't take a genius to figure out what was going on."

Harris had thought he'd seen the same thing in Melanie's eyes, but now he'd been wrong about her more than once. "That's pretty much over."

"Such a shame. I really thought you two had something there." Della covered his hand with her own. "One thing I've learned after being married for more than thirty-five years is that nothing is ever smooth and easy. It's how you deal with the bumps you hit that makes a difference."

He thought about the Kingstons, and how he'd just been thinking about their future and the bumps they would encounter. They had gone through more than many people faced in their lifetimes, yet still found a way back to each other.

"I don't know Melanie well," Della went on, "but I get the sense that she's a girl with a big heart, who is afraid to trust other people with it."

"She lied to me, Della. To get the story about John and his family."

"And did you give her a chance to explain?" Della arched a brow. "I saw the two of you arguing at the fund-raiser. And it didn't look like Melanie got a word in edgewise."

"Well…" The protest died in his throat. He'd done the same thing today that he had done eleven years ago.

Confronted her and walked away. Hadn't Melanie accused him of doing exactly that?

Maybe he hadn't changed all that much, after all. Maybe he was still leaping to conclusions instead of hearing her out.

And maybe he kept doing that because he was afraid of what he might hear if he took the time to listen.

"Some of us run from the very thing we want most in the world. And some of us undermine it because we're afraid to take that risk. Life is about risk, Harris. It's what gives a little spice to the plain every day." Della gave Harris's hand a squeeze before releasing him. "Don't give up. She's as smitten with you as you are with her."

He chuckled. "Smitten? That's a word I haven't heard in a long time."

"Just because it's an old word doesn't mean it doesn't apply to modern times." Della gathered the receipts into a pile, then got to her feet. "Anyway, it was nice chatting with you, Harris, but I really need to get home. Bobby texted me and told me he has a romantic evening planned." She beamed, as *smitten* as a teenage girl with her husband of more than three decades.

Harris seemed doomed to be surrounded by couples in love. Maybe there was something in the air around here, or at least everywhere but in the air between him and Mellie. "Good night, Della. Thank you for the advice."

"Anytime." She crossed to the door then turned back. "Oh, and Harris? There's a piece of raspberry cheesecake left in the fridge. Someone told me that's her favorite dessert. You might want to bring that with you upstairs and leave it as a surprise."

After Della left, Harris thought about her words for a long time. He opened the fridge, stared at the cheese-cake, then shut the door again.

Melanie stayed up late, writing and rewriting the article before she emailed it to Saul. For the first time in forever, a sense of pride filled her when she looked at her words. She'd been fair and honest, with a lit-tle heartstring pulling sprinkled among the facts. The email and its attachment left her out-box, and she whis-pered a prayer that it would all work out for the good.

This was it. Her new start. Her new career.

And the end of her relationship with Harris.

The wedding was only a few days away, and then she could go back to New York and put him in her past. Again. Maybe it wouldn't hurt so much the sec-ond time.

The next night, Melanie went to dinner at her sis-ter's house again and pretended to be inordinately inter-ested in the details about the flowers and the catering. She helped Abby pick out the appetizers and decide on some handmade decorations for the tables in the park, promising to come by the next day to assemble them.

She played Legos with Jake, attempted to master *Grand Theft Auto* on Cody's Xbox, and all in all, pulled off a pretty great fake-happy night. Abby gave her sister a tight hug when the evening drew to a close. "I'm glad you came over."

"Me, too. I'll be here tomorrow, around noon?"

"Sure. That would be great." Abby hugged her again.

Ma put a hand on Melanie's arm as she headed for the door. "Can we talk for a minute?"

"Sure." The two of them headed outside and began to walk the tree-lined street where Abby lived. There was a slight breeze in the air, the temps a little cooler now, edging toward fall. But it was still warm enough not to need a coat as they caught sight of the sun sinking beyond the horizon.

"Abby tells me you lost your job, too."

Melanie nodded. "And I didn't tell you about that, either, Ma. I should have, and I'm sorry."

Her mother kept walking for a while, not saying anything. "You were right about me. I do criticize and judge. I just…I wanted a different life for you girls."

"Different than the one you had as a single mom." Melanie grabbed a leaf off a low-hanging branch and tore it apart, piece by piece, watching the trail of green confetti.

Her mother nodded. "It was hard. I didn't have a college education, like the two of you do. I worked a lot of jobs that didn't pay well, and I guess I…I was angry and resentful. And I took it out on the two of you."

Ma started walking again, holding her peace for a long while. The breeze skated through the trees, making the leaves dance and chatter above them. "I went to that fund-raiser and met that newspaper editor. He raved about you. Then I read your article on the oldest living resident. I had no idea you could write with such…heart."

"Thanks." The praise warmed Melanie. Maybe because it was the first honest praise she'd heard from her mother in a long, long time. Praise that she had earned, with her words, with her work. With honest work.

Ma stopped beside a wrought iron bench. "Let me sit a little while."

Melanie realized how much older her mother had gotten in the last few years. Ma was in her late fifties now, and the years were beginning to creep into her face, her pace. Melanie settled beside her mother, feeling an odd sense of protectiveness come over her.

"Do you think it's too late for me to get really involved with the wedding? I mean, with more than my opinion?" her mother asked. "I've let Abby down so much with that."

"Of course it's not too late. Abby would love that."

Ma's features trembled, and her eyes welled. "You and Abby have always been so close. So very, very close. And I was…jealous."

"Jealous?"

Her mother drew in a breath. "When your father died, all I had was you two. It was like you and your sister became your own little unit and I was left out of that circle. Then you both moved away, and…"

Tears shimmered on her mother's lashes. For the first time, Melanie saw the vulnerability beneath her mother's strong facade, the emotions that had kept her from getting close to her daughters, that had her using criticism as a wall between them. There were hundreds of comments Melanie could retread, but she was tired of going over the past. And tired of the past controlling her future.

Melanie reached out and hugged her mother, hugged her tight, until the sun finished setting and the wounds between them began to heal.

Chapter Thirteen

Harris put all his energies into hammering, plastering and painting. He spent the next five days pouring himself into building the new Kingston home. Every day, John showed up for a few hours before and after working in his barbershop, working side by side with Harris. In the hours while they worked and sweated, Harris and John talked. The conversation in the café was forgotten, and they slipped back into their friendship without missing a step. Harris liked that, liked it a lot. John served as part father figure, part best friend, and right now, Harris needed both.

John told him about his difficult childhood, about the stresses of business ownership, about how he loved the customers he had at the barbershop. Harris opened up about his father, about the toll working with him had taken on Harris and about how he'd been searching for ways to make it up to the people he'd hurt ever since.

"Sometimes it all works out as it's meant to," John said. "I never would have settled in this town, or opened up my barbershop, if I still had the machining business. I miss my company and the people I worked with, but there's a lot less stress nowadays, where all I have to worry about is what size clipper blade to use." He nodded toward the trio of men who were shingling the new garage. "And you employing these local folks who were unemployed was a really good thing."

"I'm glad to do it, and I'm already working on some training and contacts for your people up north," Harris said. He'd changed a few lives, but it was never enough. The guilt hung on his shoulders like an unwelcome dinner guest. If Harris hadn't quit working for his father, or stayed in the same town, maybe his mother would have held on longer, or at least she wouldn't have been alone at the end. He'd never have that answer, and somehow, he needed to be okay with that. "My father has cost me and the people I care about too much. I don't want him to do that anymore."

"Cost you, like with Melanie?" John handed Harris a couple of nails, then waited while Harris used them to put a railing in place for the back deck. "You told me one night that breaking up with her was the biggest mistake of your life."

"No. Getting involved with her again was the biggest mistake of my life." He slammed the hammer head against the nail, sinking it in one move.

John picked up their water bottles and handed Harris one. "You're talking about the article."

Harris stepped back from the railing and tucked the hammer into his tool belt. He took a sip of water, but the icy liquid did nothing to quench the burn in his chest. "I told her a hundred times I didn't want the fire to be publicized. But she wrote about it anyway."

John considered that for a moment, turning the nails over and over in his palm. "Maybe because it was a story that should be told."

"I disagree." He capped the water bottle and set it back on the decking. "I can't believe she did that after I clearly asked her not to."

One of the Barlow brothers called out a break for lunch. John dropped the nails back into the bucket but reached for Harris's shoulder to stop him from leaving. "Have you even read it?"

"No." He'd heard that Saul had sent it on to the *Charlotte Observer*. The piece came out this morning, and Harris had no doubt that by this afternoon, reporters would be swarming the job site. He'd already had several calls from unknown numbers that he had let go straight to voice mail.

"Then you don't know if she was kind or cruel. You don't know if maybe…maybe she's written a piece that could change someone else's life. Stop a man from picking up a drink when he really should be picking up the phone." John's voice roughened. "Catherine and I read it, and I have to say, I think she did a wonderful job capturing the story."

Harris considered this. "I expected her to write some

exploitive piece that would get her picked up by a national news outlet."

"Yeah, well, you thought wrong." John reached in his back pocket and pulled out a folded paper. "See for yourself."

Harris stared at the newsprint, half-afraid to open it up.

John clapped Harris on the back. "We all make mistakes, Harris. We lose our judgment, we leap without looking, we hurt the ones we love. But if our motives are true, then we know we've done the best we can—or at least, that we'll try to do better in the future. I don't know Melanie, but my wife thinks she's amazing because she's been here, helping out. She's called and checked on Catherine every day. She dropped off school supplies and backpacks for the kids yesterday. Someone like that wouldn't write an article that would hurt my family."

Mellie had done all of that? He knew she'd been at the job site off and on, mostly whenever he wasn't here, because Jack Barlow had mentioned it. But he had no idea she had been so involved with the Kingstons.

John went off to eat lunch while Harris stayed behind with the half-finished railing and the story Mellie had written. The exterior of the new Kingston family home was up, and the interior walls were beginning to take shape. Plumbing and electrical were snaking through the frame, laying a blueprint for a new beginning. The entire site looked and smelled like a fresh start. A do-over for one bad decision.

Maybe it was time Harris did the same.

* * *

Melanie started to cry when she slid the zipper up Abby's back. "God, you look so beautiful. And so happy."

Abby beamed at her reflection. Her dress was simple, white and knee-length, with cap sleeves and a scoop neck and a small ring of rhinestones around the hem. She'd forgone a veil, leaving her dark hair long and held back with a barrette decorated with tiny flowers and long, slender ribbons that trailed down to her shoulders. "It's like I'm seventeen again and going to the prom with the cool guy. Except this time I get to stay with him for the rest of my life."

Melanie hugged Abby, a light embrace to avoid wrinkling her dress. "Dylan's a lucky guy."

"So is Harris—or at least, he will be soon, once he gets his head on straight." Abby reached for two bouquets of lilies, one small for Melanie, and one big for herself, then handed Melanie her flowers.

"Harris? We're not even dating."

"Then why have you been moping around the last few days?" Abby arched a brow. "You've been here almost every day, saying you're helping me get ready for the wedding—"

"Which I did. I made all those Mason jars with the flowers in them and decorated those big candles for the tables. At least I didn't have to outfit a baby goat, too."

The joke flickered in Abby's smile, then disappeared. "And the whole time, you looked like you had lost your best friend." Her features softened. "Why don't you go talk to him?"

"Because I betrayed him and I don't think he will forgive me." She sighed and plopped into the chair in Abby's bedroom. "I wrote that story about the Kingstons and sent it to Saul. For five minutes, I dreamed of a big paper picking it up and being able to use it to launch my career again and get the fund-raiser a lot of publicity and donations. Then I thought of Harris's face when he confronted me, and I...I couldn't do it. I called Saul and begged him not to run it, but he told me it was too good to let it sit in a drawer. He called the *Charlotte Observer*, and they ran it this morning."

"I know. Ma brought me the paper early this morning. She bought ten of them, in fact." Abby grinned. "She's a little proud. And so am I. It was a beautiful piece, Melanie."

"Which means nothing if I hurt someone I love by writing it." As soon as the words were out, Melanie realized they were true. She did love Harris. She had never stopped, not really. But what she'd done had ruined any chance between them, and there was no taking that moment back.

So she helped her sister get ready and drove down to the park to meet the minister and Dylan and the boys, who had spent the night with their soon-to-be stepfather. The Barlow family was there, along with Mavis and Dylan's uncle Ty and a bunch of other families from town. She noticed the Kingstons sitting in the fourth row, the kids wearing the new clothes she had gone with Catherine to buy a couple days ago.

The minister stepped into the center of the makeshift outdoor church setting, and a band began to play

Abby and Dylan's favorite song, while Abby's boys walked her down the aisle to Dylan. Melanie saw Ma crying in the front row. Abby stopped, leaned down, hugged her mother, and the two shared a moment before Abby straightened and met her husband-to-be at the end of the rows of chairs. The boys peeled off to sit by their grandmother, and the minister began to speak.

Melanie barely heard the words her sister and Dylan spoke. All she saw was the love radiating between them, the happiness. It almost glowed. A swell of envy grew in Melanie, as she saw what could be—if she found true love.

Once upon a time, she'd thought she had that with Harris. But in typical Melanie fashion, she had detonated it all by keeping the truth from him. Taken off, headed to school—

Running.

Wasn't that what she had done all week, too? Run from seeing him? Avoided him, instead of going to him and having a heart-to-heart about the article, about how she felt, about what had scared her all those years ago?

The ceremony came to an end, Abby and Dylan kissed, and the crowd cheered. They headed over to the park gazebo where the band was set up and a couple dozen tables and chairs were decorated for the guests. Jack Barlow had constructed a temporary dance floor, and as soon as the band began to play, Dylan waltzed onto it with his bride.

Melanie laid the bouquets on one of the tables and hung to the side, under the shade of a tree, watching them and thinking about how her life could have gone differently if only she had stayed put and talked instead of avoided.

Saul came over to her. The perpetual ball cap was still on his head, even though he'd dressed up and added a tie to his usual short-sleeve button-down shirt. "Nice wedding."

"It was. Nice and casual. Great to see so many people from town here."

Saul nodded. "And the Kingstons. I heard from Mrs. K that you bought their dress clothes for today and took their little one to get a suit."

She'd used the money she'd earned from writing for the *Stone Gap Gazette*, which still put her behind the eight ball financially, but the look of gratitude on Catherine Kingston's face made it worth the expense. "It was the least I could do. They're such a wonderful family."

"And a part of you feels like a jerk for writing that article?" Saul arched a brow.

"Yeah." Even though the family had loved the article, Melanie still felt terrible. The *Observer* had called her this morning, offering her a job as a staff reporter. So had two other big-city papers and one national magazine. She'd let all the calls go to voice mail.

"Well, don't. That article is one of the best damned pieces of journalism I have seen in a long time. And I've been around since the Stone Age, so I should know. My friend at the *Observer* said he called and offered you a job. You should take it. They're a great paper to work for and can pay a lot more than I could. My fishing will just have to wait a bit."

It was everything she'd wanted, all wrapped up with a tidy little bow. And yet she felt more depressed than she had when her life fell apart.

The old Melanie would have said to hell with the consequences, just run the article and she'd be on her way before the fallout had a chance to hit. But this was the new Melanie, the one who had grown up a lot in the last year, and who had finally realized that being honest with those she loved—and with herself—was the only way forward. And this Melanie couldn't ignore the havoc she'd created in her path of best intentions.

"I'm thinking about his offer," she said. "I haven't decided what I want to do yet."

"I get that. But you know…"

"A job offer like that won't be there forever." She gave Saul a smile. "Thank you for believing in me."

"It was easy to do after I read your work. And for the record, I'm eating more kale now, too." He grinned.

She laughed. "Well, that's got to be good for you."

"And my cellulite." He winked, then said goodbye and headed back to the party.

Melanie watched her sister dancing with Cody, while Dylan hoisted Jacob into his arms and took a spin on the dance floor. John asked Catherine to dance, and she slipped into his arms like she'd always been there.

Out of the corner of her eye, Melanie saw Harris, striding across the wide green lawn of the park. He had on a navy suit and red floral tie, which made her pulse race. Damn, he looked good in a suit. Even better with a tie. It had been a long time since she'd seen him this dressed up, and the effect nearly made her come undone. God, it was going to be hard to leave him again. And twice as hard to forget him this time.

He greeted a few people he knew as he made his way through the crowd in the reception and then over to her. As they had from the day she arrived, the people of Stone Gap welcomed Harris with open arms. Instead of pausing to talk, he kept going, straight toward her. She held her breath, not quite sure what she wanted to say to him yet, but knowing it was a long-overdue conversation.

"You look beautiful," he said.

She smiled. "Thank you. You still do a suit justice. I haven't seen you in one in a long time."

"Thanks." He nodded toward the dance floor. "I'm sorry I missed the ceremony, but Abby and Dylan look really happy."

Small talk. It filled the space between them. "They are. They really are. And I'm glad. My sister has had a tough life, and she deserves that fairy tale."

"Everyone does," he said.

Did he mean her? And him? Or was she looking for something that wasn't there? And when was she going to grow up and stop hoping for the impossible?

"I have something I should have told you a long time ago," Melanie said. She was done keeping secrets, done running from the truth. Not just with her sister and mother, but with everyone in her life. "It won't change anything about today, but still, you should know. Can we take a little walk?"

"Sure."

Melanie waved to Abby, mouthing that she'd be

right back. Abby nodded and gave her sister a little thumbs-up.

They walked across the park and away from the crowded wedding reception. When the music from the band was in the distant background, she began to speak. "You were right when you accused me of lying when we broke up. I wasn't lying when I said I wasn't involved with Dave. I did lie about why he was there. And why I needed a hug from him." She drew in a deep breath. "I got pregnant."

He stopped walking. His jaw dropped. "You did?"

She could see him doing the math in his head, the questions about the baby, and then the sorrow filling his eyes when he realized there was no ten-year-old child standing between them. She nodded, and even now, a decade later, the loss still seared her chest and filled her eyes. "I lost it the day before we broke up. I had only found out a couple days before, and was still getting used to the idea, and trying to figure out how to tell you. But then I woke up one morning in terrible pain. I kept hoping it wasn't true, that the cramps and the bleeding were normal, but then I went to the doctor, and he confirmed it. I was devastated. When I left the office, Dave was walking by, and the whole story just poured out of me. What you saw was a friend comforting a friend who had lost something she already loved. Not a relationship I was keeping a secret."

"Why didn't you tell me?"

"You never gave me a chance. You freaked out, broke up with me and left. I was so hurt that you would think I was cheating that I didn't call you to try to explain. And I was angry that you weren't there to help me get through the worst days of my life. The very person I needed was the one who had caused me so much of that pain." She let out a breath. "So I signed up for college and got out of town the first chance I had. I vowed to forget all about you, and that summer, and most of all, that night." She swiped at her eyes. When Harris came closer, she put up a hand. If she didn't get it all out now, she never would. "I felt like such a failure. The one thing I should have been able to do, that millions of women do every year, and I...I screwed it up." She shook her head and willed the tears in her eyes not to fall. "I know now that it wasn't my fault, that sometimes those things just happen. But back then, I saw myself as a failure, and I didn't want to be that anymore. So I went to college, and I moved to New York, and I got the job that, at the time, seemed glamorous and exciting and married the man every other woman thought was amazing. And then I lost it all." She sighed. "I failed again, and I couldn't bring myself to tell anyone the truth."

"No, you didn't fail. You went after your dreams, and you picked yourself up, and you did it again."

"At your expense." She cupped his face with her hand and stared into the brown eyes she had loved most of her life. She knew now why she hadn't rushed to send the article in to the paper. Why she had hesitated on letting Saul run it. Why she hadn't taken the job with the Charlotte paper. "I begged Saul not to run that story. I didn't want to hurt you. Or the family."

"You didn't." Harris reached into his jacket and

pulled out the folded newspaper. "John gave me a copy, and I read it just now. It was…beautiful, Mellie. I knew the story and I still got caught up in the emotions. You were fair and honest and so very considerate of the Kingstons and what they have been through."

She had been waiting for the disapproval. The anger. His pride and praise floored her. "You…you liked it?"

"No. I loved it. You're so incredibly talented, Mellie." Harris shifted closer to her. "I should have known that you would be fair. That you would be the only reporter I could truly trust."

"And yet you've never trusted me."

"Because you are a very powerful woman, Melanie Cooper." He tipped her chin until she was looking at him. "From the day I met you, you've been the only one in the world who could break my heart. And that terrified me."

She scoffed. "I don't think anything terrifies you, Harris."

"The thought of losing you does. I went through that once. I don't want to do it again." He caught her hands in his and drew her to his chest. "Even after I left town and quit working for him, my father was ruling my life. He never approved of us dating."

"I remember. He wanted you to date some other girl."

"The daughter of a business associate. An alliance that would benefit him, I'm sure, just like he benefited from the closing of John's business and all the other people whose lives he ruined." Harris shook his head.

"I spent too many years trying to get the approval of someone I don't even like. And all it did was cost me."

She was close to him, so close that she could catch the scent of his cologne. So close that her heart ached for more. Ached for him to tell her to stay. But she had made it clear a hundred times that this was just a temporary thing, and after today, she'd be going back to New York and he'd be going back to his life. Better to be strong now, get it over with, before she began to cry. "I'm glad we had a chance to see each other again before I leave."

"Don't." His gaze met hers. "Don't walk out of my life again, Mellie."

There was a hitch of vulnerability in the way he said her name, the touch of his hand. Her heart melted and she lifted her chin until she was close enough to kiss him. "Why?"

"Because I love you. I always have."

"You still love me?"

He nodded. "I knew it the second I saw you again. It was like we'd said goodbye yesterday, not a decade ago."

Joy soared inside her. She'd tried so hard to be practical, to keep her heart out of all of this, but her love for him had been in every word of the article she wrote. "I felt the same. I was just so scared. I mean, I don't want to screw this up, Harris."

"You won't." He brushed a tendril of hair off her forehead. "Because this time, both of us are staying put."

"Here?"

"Seems like a great town to make a new beginning in, don't you think?"

Melanie turned and looked at the people gathered for Abby's wedding. The warm circle that surrounded her sister and their family. How she had been welcomed into Stone Gap as if she'd always belonged here. She had never really felt that in Connecticut or in New York. But here, with the coconut cream pie and the exploding pink dress shop, she had found home. "It does."

"Then let's do that, Mellie." He gathered her into his arms and kissed her—a long, deep, sweet kiss that made her heart melt and made her want more. Much more. "I love you."

"I love you, too, Harris." She raised her gaze to his. "Does this mean we get to write a new ending to our story?"

"It does indeed. But I think we're going to need to buy some more legal pads first." He kissed her again and again, until she was breathless. "Because I intend to have one long, happy life with you."

"That sounds like the perfect ending to me." She leaned into his arms and watched the sun set, the lights come on and a new life begin in the middle of Stone Gap.

She couldn't have written it better if she tried.

* * * * *

Look for the next book in
New York Times *bestselling author*
Shirley Jump's miniseries,
The Stone Gap Inn.

Available November 2019,
wherever Harlequin Special Edition
books and ebooks are sold.

COMING NEXT MONTH FROM

H HARLEQUIN®

SPECIAL EDITION

Available August 20, 2019

#2713 THE MAVERICK'S WEDDING WAGER
Montana Mavericks: Six Brides for Six Brothers
by Joanna Sims
To escape his father's matchmaking schemes, wealthy rancher Knox Crawford announces a whirlwind wedding to local Genevieve Lawrence. But his very real bride turns out to be more than he bargained for—especially when fake marriage leads to real love!

#2714 HOME TO BLUE STALLION RANCH
Men of the West • by Stella Bagwell
Isabelle Townsend is finally living out her dream of raising horses on the ranch she just purchased in Arizona. But when she clashes with Holt Hollister, the sparks that result could have them both making room in their lives for a new dream.

#2715 THE MARINE'S FAMILY MISSION
Camden Family Secrets • by Victoria Pade
Marine Declan Madison was there for some of the worst—and best—moments of Emmy Tate's life. So when he shows up soon after she's taken custody of her nieces, Emmy isn't sure how to feel. But their attraction can't be ignored... Can Declan get things right this time around?

#2716 A MAN YOU CAN TRUST
Gallant Lake Stories • by Jo McNally
After escaping her abusive ex, Cassie Smith is thankful for a job and a safe place to stay at the Gallant Lake Resort. Nick West makes her nervous with his restless energy, but when he starts teaching her self-defense, Cassie begins to see a future that involves roots and community. But can Nick let go of his own difficult past to give Cassie the freedom she needs?

#2717 THIS TIME FOR KEEPS
Wickham Falls Weddings • by Rochelle Alers
Attorney Nicole Campos hasn't spoken to local mechanic Fletcher Austen since their high school friendship went down in flames over a decade ago. But when her car breaks down during her return to Wickham Falls and Fletcher unexpectedly helps her out with a custody situation in court, they find themselves suddenly wondering if this time is for keeps...

#2718 WHEN YOU LEAST EXPECT IT
The Culhanes of Cedar River • by Helen Lacey
Tess Fuller dreamed of being a mother—but never that one memorable night with her ex-husband would lead to a baby! Despite their shared heartbreak, take-charge rancher Mitch Culhane hasn't ever stopped loving Tess. Now he has the perfect solution: marriage, take two. But unless he can prove he's changed, Tess isn't so sure their love story can have a happily-ever-after...

YOU CAN FIND MORE INFORMATION ON UPCOMING HARLEQUIN® TITLES,
FREE EXCERPTS AND MORE AT WWW.HARLEQUIN.COM.

HSECNM0819

Get 4 FREE REWARDS!

We'll send you 2 FREE Books plus 2 FREE Mystery Gifts.

Harlequin® Special Edition books feature heroines finding the balance between their work life and personal life on the way to finding true love.

FREE
Value Over
$20

YES! Please send me 2 FREE Harlequin® Special Edition novels and my 2 FREE gifts (gifts are worth about $10 retail). After receiving them, if I don't wish to receive any more books, I can return the shipping statement marked "cancel." If I don't cancel, I will receive 6 brand-new novels every month and be billed just $4.99 per book in the U.S. or $5.74 per book in Canada. That's a savings of at least 12% off the cover price! It's quite a bargain! Shipping and handling is just 50¢ per book in the U.S. and $1.25 per book in Canada.* I understand that accepting the 2 free books and gifts places me under no obligation to buy anything. I can always return a shipment and cancel at any time. The free books and gifts are mine to keep no matter what I decide.

235/335 HDN GNMP

Name (please print)

Address   Apt. #

City   State/Province   Zip/Postal Code

Mail to the **Reader Service:**
IN U.S.A.: P.O. Box 1341, Buffalo, NY 14240-8531
IN CANADA: P.O. Box 603, Fort Erie, Ontario L2A 5X3

Want to try 2 free books from another series? Call 1-800-873-8635 or visit www.ReaderService.com.

"Why are you armed with pepper spray? Did something happen to you?"

She didn't look up.

"Yes. Something happened."

"Here?"

She shook her head, her body trembling so badly she didn't trust her voice. The only sound was Nick's wheezing breath. He finally cleared his throat.

"Okay. Something happened." His voice was gravelly from the pepper spray, but it was calmer than it had been a few minutes ago. "And you wanted to protect yourself. That's smart. But you need to do it right. I'll teach you."

Her head snapped up. He was doing his best to look at her, even though his left eye was still closed.

"What are you talking about?"

"I'll teach you self-defense, Cassie. The kind that actually works."

"Are you talking karate or something? I thought the pepper spray…"

"It's a tool, but you need more than that. If some guy's amped up on drugs, he'll just be temporarily blinded and really ticked off." He picked up the pepper spray canister from the grass at her side. "This stuff will spray up to ten feet away. You never should have let me get so close before using it."

"I didn't know that."

"Exactly." He grimaced and swore again. "I need to get home and dunk my face in a bowl full of ice water." He stood and reached a hand down to help her up. She hesitated, then took it.

Don't miss
A Man You Can Trust *by Jo McNally,*
available September 2019 wherever
Harlequin® Special Edition books and ebooks are sold.

www.Harlequin.com

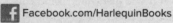

Meg tensed from head to toe, sucking in her breath as she
saw two masculine hands close over the shutters' edges on
either side of her body. Then instinctively turned her head to
take in light hair, a strong stubbled jaw and blue eyes—no
more than an inch from hers.

"I... I..." He smelled good. Not sweaty at all, the way
she surely did. The firm muscles in his arms bracketed her
shoulders.

"I think I got it if you just wanna kinda duck down under
my arm." Despite the awkward situation and the weight of
the shutter, the suggestion came out sounding entirely good-
natured.

And okay, yes, separating their bodies was an excellent
idea. Because she wasn't accustomed to being pressed up
against any other guy besides Zack, for any reason, not even
practical ones. And a stranger to boot. Who on earth was this
guy, and how had he just magically materialized in her yard?

The ducking-under-his-arm part kept her feeling just as
awkward as the rest of the contact until it was accomplished.
And when she finally freed herself, her rescuer calmly,

competently lowered the loose shutter to the ground, leaning it against the house with an easy "There we go."

He wore a snug black T-shirt that showed his well-muscled torso—though she already knew about that part from having felt it against her back. Just below the sleeve she caught sight of a tattoo—some sort of swirling design inked on his left biceps. His sandy hair could have used a trim, and something about him gave off an air of modern-day James Dean.

"Um… I…" Wow. He'd really taken her aback. Normally she could converse with people she didn't know—she did it all summer every year at the inn. But then, this had been no customary meeting. Even now that she stood a few feet away, she still felt the heat of his body cocooning her as it had a moment ago.

That was when he shifted his gaze from the shutter to her face, flashing a disarming grin.

That was when she took in the crystalline quality of his eyes, shining on her like a couple of blue marbles, or maybe it was more the perfect clear blue of faraway seas.

That was when she realized…he was younger than her, notably so. But hotter than the day was long. And so she gave up trying to speak entirely and settled on just letting a quiet sigh echo out, hoping her unbidden reactions to him didn't show.

Need to know what happens next?
Find out when you order your copy of
The One Who Stays *by Toni Blake,*
available August 2019 wherever you buy your books!

www.Harlequin.com

Love Harlequin romance?

DISCOVER.

Be the first to find out about promotions, news and exclusive content!

f Facebook.com/HarlequinBooks

Twitter.com/HarlequinBooks

Instagram.com/HarlequinBooks

Pinterest.com/HarlequinBooks

ReaderService.com

EXPLORE.

Sign up for the Harlequin e-newsletter and download a free book from any series at **TryHarlequin.com.**

CONNECT.

Join our Harlequin community to share your thoughts and connect with other romance readers! **Facebook.com/groups/HarlequinConnection**

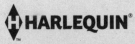

HARLEQUIN®

ROMANCE WHEN YOU NEED IT

HSOCIAL2018